PARANORMAL COZY MYSTERY

Bars & Boxcars

TRIXIE SILVERTALE

Sittin' On A Goldmine
Productions L.L.C.

Sittin' On A Goldmine Productions, L.L.C.

pr@sittinonagoldmine.co

www.sittinonagoldmine.co

This is a work of fiction. Names, characters, places, and incidents are products of the author's imagination or are used fictitiously and are not to be construed as real. Any resemblance to actual events, locales, business establishments, organizations, or persons, living or dead, is entirely coincidental.

ISBN: 978-1-952739-60-6

Cover Design © Sittin' On A Goldmine Productions, L.L.C.

Trixie Silvertale
Bars and Boxcars: Paranormal Cozy Mystery : a novel / by Trixie Silvertale — 1st ed.

[1. Paranormal Cozy Mystery — Fiction. 2. Cozy Mystery — Fiction. 3. Amateur Sleuths — Fiction. 4. Female Sleuth — Fiction. 5. Wit and Humor — Fiction.] 1. Title.

CHAPTER 1

I'M NOT THE kind of person that gets excited about grand openings. But this one is special for a couple of reasons. The first is that I'm less than a year into building a relationship with my long-lost father, and this event marks the realization of his dream project. So, of course, I'm way supportive of that.

The second reason is slightly more complicated. As a newly minted heiress this is kind of like my quinceañera, or maybe my debutante ball. I'll be rubbing elbows with the wealthiest and most influential people in my new hometown of Pin Cherry Harbor. Which is not something a broke-as-*Little-Women*, ex-barista from Sedona, Arizona, ever imagined.

In light of these stakes, I'll attempt to keep my unpredictable psychic powers under control and "act" normal. If I receive any supernatural messages, I will remain calm and carry on.

Tonight's event is the official launch of the Duncan Restorative Justice Foundation. Despite the setback of a towering inferno a few months ago, which destroyed the original historic building, my father, Jacob Duncan, made a grand gesture to the Pin Cherry Historical Society to get on their good side and fast-track his build.

I'm learning all sorts of things about how grand gestures (a.k.a. large donations) make the world go 'round.

His new headquarters is a miniature replica of the most famous building in all of Birch County: City Hall. A picture-perfect structure that reminds me of a scene from *To Kill a Mockingbird*. The original, in the town square, stands about fifty feet tall. Three stories of solid granite with copper parapet walls, featuring original terrazzo floors, ornamental plaster cornices, and marble walls at the elevator lobby. It's truly the height of architectural design in Pin Cherry.

My father recreated all of these details in his pricey, post-fire redesign. Even though his site has a smaller footprint, there are still three lovely stories. In addition, he went the extra mile and added a historical marker with a large bronze plaque commemorating the original Iron Range Brewing Company building that was destroyed by the blaze. The marker appears on the official Historical Society guide map and gives a brief account of the legend of the brewery.

Now, the building that was burned to ash was the part of the complex that served as the sleeping quarters and the stables. The structure that once housed the distillery portion of the brewery is still standing next door and is home to the Bell, Book & Candle Bookshop, left to me by my eccentric late grandmother.

When I say "late," it's not as though she actually crossed over. Not even close! The ghost of my wonderful grandmother, Myrtle Isadora, is tethered to the bookshop—permanently—as near as I can tell. Plus, there's the added bonus that her incredibly spoiled fur baby, a tan caracal, named Pyewacket, was also left in my care.

"Mitzy!" My father grins anxiously and waves me over. I do my best to walk like a lady in my vintage couture and Manolo Blahniks, also courtesy of Grams. But it's not easy, when my normal wardrobe consists of skinny jeans, T-shirts, and canvas high-tops.

My dad runs a nervous hand through his freshly trimmed bone-white blond hair, which mirrors my own. However, my white hair is currently twisted within an inch of its life by Ghost-ma and pinned into place with a million bobby pins.

I give him an encouraging wink and witness a flicker of gratitude in his thoughtful grey eyes. We also share our eye color; my eyes just happen to be more mischievous than contemplative. "Hey, Dad, looks like a pretty great turnout. How are you holding up?"

He straightens his blue necktie and tugs on the sleeves of his suit jacket. "I think there's a saying about long-tailed cats and rocking chairs, but I can't remember it right now, and I feel like I might sweat through everything I'm wearing in ten seconds flat." He swallows audibly and struggles to take a deep breath. "Is the statue of my father too much?"

"Of course not. It was a thoughtful gesture."

I pat him on the back and he exhales a sigh of relief.

I can hardly tell him how I really feel about the huge bronze replica of my recently deceased grandfather—a man I never met. The sight of the larger-than-life likeness gives me the heebie-jeebies! The one and only time I ever saw Cal Duncan was as a corpse, the first day I arrived in Pin Cherry. That was also the first time the handsome local sheriff accused me of murder. But that's another story, and I need to focus on keeping my dad calm. "Don't worry, it'll be over soon."

"I can tell you one thing, sweetie. When I was sitting in that prison cell in the Clearwater State Penitentiary, I never imagined I'd be hosting a fundraiser swarming with judges and lawyers."

Before I can respond with a clever quip, one of those lawyers sidles up next to us, stretches up on her tiptoes, and plants a big kiss on my father's cheek.

Amaryllis, my late grandfather's former lawyer and my dad's current main squeeze, slips an arm around his waist and leans into his chest as she whispers, "Relax. You look wonderful. You're a wealthy, influential philanthropist. Utterly above reproach." She lowers her voice, and I have to rely on my extrasensory perception to actually hear her final comment. "And I love you."

My father blushes and averts his gaze.

I can't keep the *Saturday Night Live* refrain from playing inside my head. "You're good enough, you're smart enough, and doggone it, people like you!" Luckily, I've matured enough in the last year to keep this nugget to myself.

Amaryllis adjusts her red-brown locks and gives me a friendly wink and a pat on the shoulder as she dives back into the fray, to press the flesh and greet the guests.

I knew she and my father were getting close, but I wasn't aware that "love" was on the table. The little girl in me that lost her mom in a terrible accident when she was eleven and spent over six years in the foster system flares with jealousy. However, the twenty-two-year-old, who's building a new life in a small town hugging the shores of a great lake in almost-Canada, is really happy for my dad.

"Good evening, Mizithra."

The somber voice of my curmudgeonly lawyer and mentor, Silas Willoughby, calls me back from my trip down memory lane.

"Silas. Can you believe this turnout? This has to be all Amaryllis's doing. You and I both know my dad did not call these judges!"

He chuckles. "I, too, was pleased to offer some assistance. Perhaps you've forgotten how long I've been a barrister in this county."

"How could I possibly forget?" Honestly, he's constantly reminding me of his vast experience, and my need to take things more seriously and listen to his advice. "Thank you for coming, Silas. If you get a chance, give Grams a little wave. She's swirling frantically in front of the six-by-six windows in my apartment next door. She wanted you to figure out some way to allow her access to this building, but I told her she was being greedy and that an important alchemist-attorney, such as yourself, has better things to do."

He harrumphs into his grey mustache and

smooths it with his thumb and forefinger. "Indeed. That woman is always tempting fate for just one more obligement."

I inhale deeply, square my shoulders and say, "I guess it's time to be my dad's wingman. I can only imagine how uncomfortable he must be tonight." I swallow my own discomfort and add, "That being said, I do believe his program to help wrongly convicted inmates overturn their convictions and provide good-paying, legal employment for ex-cons will truly pay off."

"That speech should secure several new donations. You are a virtuous daughter. And a meritorious friend." Silas nods his bald head and his jowls waggle as he waves to an acquaintance across the room.

I stuff down my virtue-related retort, grab a glass of champagne off the passing tray, and paste on a five-star smile.

Moving through the crowd, I'm nearly overcome with the unpleasant mix of yesteryear's aftershave, stale cigar smoke, and something that must be a muscle liniment. I catch snippets of terribly uninteresting conversation. Until I hear this: "Well, of course I told him, you absolutely can see the Great Wall of China from space. I heard it from Buzz Aldrin myself." I stutter step to a stop and pretend to search the crowd. This small, self-important judge seems to be holding court, and not a single member of his rapt audience bothers to contradict him.

I'm not in a rocket ship touring space, hoping to see the Great Wall, so I couldn't care less what he tells them. I'm not the one who is going to be disappointed, certainly not as disappointed as my friend Rhonda who went on a booze cruise to Baja, California, for her twenty-first birthday. She got conned into taking a glass-bottom-boat tour on the Sea of Cortez and saw nothing but rocks. You pay $100 a person and you're promised sightings of all sorts of lovely tropical fish, seals, and dolphins, and instead you see—sand. Now that's legitimate disappointment.

It's not my place to correct the pompous little man, despite the satisfaction it might bring. Tonight, according to Ghost-ma's pep talk, I have to be on my best behavior.

Moving away from the temptation, I keep scanning the crowd with secret desperation. I'm sure Amaryllis invited Erick Harper, or, as I like to call him, Sheriff Too-Hot-To-Handle. However, we're two hours into this three-hour event and there's no sign of him.

I thought he'd at least show up as a personal favor to me. I mean, we've had a few casual dates and, if the fates hadn't conspired against us, we might have had an actual kiss.

Feeling forlorn, I'm about to give up hope when I see a flash of a tan uniform near the front door.

My heart does a cartwheel and the magicked heirloom mood ring on my left hand burns with an otherworldly message. I avoid looking at my ring, because every ounce of my energy is focused on making Erick—

Disappointment doesn't begin to describe the wave of emotion that washes over me. Devastation is probably closer. The tan uniform shirt belongs to none other than my least favorite deputy, Pauly Paulsen. Argh!

I once attempted to mock that name, but there's a saying about stones and glass houses. I mean, I'm named after the ball of Greek cheese that featured heavily in the meet-cute that led to my parents' one and only one-night stand.

Paulsen waddles her way through the crowd, one pudgy hand on her gun and the other pushing people aside with far more self-importance than courtesy.

Her eyes search the sea of faces. They land on me for a split-second, but, after an unnecessary eye roll, they move on.

Eventually, she sidles up to one of the many elderly white males in attendance and whispers something in his ear.

The man, who I think might be the Great Wall of China judge, follows her out of the lobby.

Now all my psychic senses are tingling.

Cops need judges for two things: search warrants and arrest warrants. I mean, there's probably other stuff, but as a film-school dropout those are the two that hit the popular movie tropes.

My ring sends a spike of heat up my hand and this time I glance at the black cabochon in time to see a section of train track, before the swirling black mist inside the glass dome swallows the image.

Deputy Paulsen. Train tracks. My dad owning the Midwest Union Railway.

Coincidence? I think not.

This town never seems to get tired of trying to pin crimes on my father!

CHAPTER 2

My ATTEMPTS TO catch up with Paulsen are stymied by these blankety-blank heels on the terrazzo flooring. It's more dangerous than trying to run on black ice. I came to know that slippery danger first hand during my premier winter up north, and it did not end well for my backside, so I'm forced to slow my pace and preserve my dignity.

Paulsen gets whatever she came for and slips out the front door. I'm left with no clue about her visit and the unsavory option of pestering a sitting judge, like the nosy Gladys Kravitz from *Bewitched*.

Now might be a good time to mention that my happy place is film and television. Those lovely worlds that unfold before the eyes saved me from oblivion during my years in foster care. Of course, the aftereffect is that I tend to draw most of my real-world comparisons from that utterly fictional universe. *Comme ci comme ça.*

Like a laser targeting system, I keep my eyes trained on the tonsured head of Paulsen's judge. If I lose him in this crowd of near-clones, I'll never find him again.

Without breaking the visual lock, I scoop a tray of champagne flutes off the bar cart and ignore the caterer's queries.

I'm closing fast. Three more strides and—

"Mitzy, I hope you're not planning on attempting what I hypothesize." Silas glides into my path like a ballroom dancer, but plants his feet with the permanence of a mighty oak.

He can be very sneaky.

My fake smile fades. My shoulders droop. I down a flute of bubbly from my own tray.

"This is your father's big night. You'll have a plethora of time to sleuth around the sheriff's station tomorrow."

The caterer finally catches up to me and unceremoniously reclaims his tray of stemware.

Leaning toward Silas, I whisper into his preternaturally large ear. "I got a message in my ring. 'Train tracks.' I'm worried Paulsen is out to get my dad again."

He nods as though he holds the wisdom and patience of the ages in either hand. "And tomorrow you will unearth the meaning beneath the message." He puts a hand on my arm and gently turns me toward the center of the room. "For the time being, you have an anxious father who needs a calm presence at his side."

Have I mentioned how much I hate it when Silas is right? "Copy that, Mr. Willoughby." I turn my Vegas-neon smile back on and catwalk across the lobby.

Despite my good intentions, Amaryllis intercepts me before I can reach my paternal destination and steers me toward the alcove housing the roped-off elevator. The image immediately reminds me of Twiggy's "No Admittance" sign blocking looky-loos from the Rare Books Loft back at my bookshop.

Amaryllis leans in conspiratorially. "Mitzy, I know we don't know each other all that well, but I have a little *situation* and rumor has it you're a bit of an amateur detective."

I nod too eagerly. "I knew it! There's something going on with the trains, isn't there?"

She gazes up at me and her eyes widen with a mix of suspicion and shock.

For the first time, I notice flecks of gold and green in her dark-brown eyes.

"So, the rumors are true?" she murmurs.

I hope she's referring to rumors about my

sleuthing and not rumors about my psychic powers. I choose to go with a noncommittal reply. "I guess."

"You get the visions, like Isadora? Jacob's always been cagey about it when I ask him, but Cal never stopped talking about how Isadora's visions were a boon and a curse. Does it drive you crazy? When do you get them?"

I wish I could formulate a response to staunch the word-vomit that she's spewing at me, but I can't even manage to close my mouth.

"Well, we don't have to talk about it right now, sweetie." She flutters her hand rapidly to indicate she's pushing the topic away and grins.

I exhale the breath I didn't know I was holding and successfully close my gaping maw.

She continues to unfurl her request. "Judge Peterson, no relation, just texted me. Sounds like Deputy Paulsen interrupted the grand opening to get his signature on a search warrant for a line of boxcars on a siding near Grand Falls."

There's so much to unpack that I have to put up my hand to give myself a moment of silence. Any mention of Grand Falls is bound to bring images of the green-eyed sidewinder Rory Bombay to mind, so I have to process that. Then there's the search warrant being issued for a train that, more than likely, originated out of my father's Midwest Union depot. And finally the tidbit about her last name being Peterson, which I don't think I actually knew. Where to begin? While I'm muddling that over, Amaryllis makes her "ask."

"Can you pump your contact at the sheriff's station for information? I'd sure like to know if they're gearing up for another assault on your father's good name."

I try to listen, I honestly do. But as soon as she says "sheriff's station," I kind of get lost in one of my mind movies. This one stars Sheriff Erick Harper and it is not rated PG.

"Mitzy? Are you having a vision right now?" She leans toward me with a mix of concern and anticipation.

Oops, I've drifted off for too long. "Yes. What? Wait, I mean, no. I mean, I'll stop by the station first thing in the morning."

She sort of nods and shakes her head at the same time. "Would you mind giving a call right now? If Paulsen was pushing for that warrant tonight . . ."

Amaryllis Peterson may stand a head shorter than me, but those dark eyes pack a wallop. I'm powerless to refuse. "I'm on it."

"Thank you. I owe you one." She strides back into the party in her tailored DKNY skirt suit without a backward glance.

Torn between the need to please my dad's girlfriend and the need to not infuriate my mentor, I struggle for a full three seconds with my decision.

Of course, I'm going to call Erick. I'm honestly a little miffed he didn't turn up.

A male deputy answers the phone and transfers me to the sheriff—whom I ask for by his proper title and with the expected amount of decorum.

"Hey, Erick, why is Deputy Paulsen interrupting my dad's grand opening party to get a search warrant signed?"

To his credit he doesn't even act surprised or enquire how I got my information. But he does attempt to sidestep my question with a boilerplate line about not discussing ongoing investigations.

Before he can shut me down completely, I hit him with the one tiny piece of knowledge I possess. "Are you searching the depot too, or are you only searching the boxcars? If you're going to try to implicate my dad in something, I think I deserve fair warning. As a—friend."

The low whistle on the other end of the line brings a smile to my face. Apparently I haven't lost all my mystery.

However, the story that Erick unravels brings a fresh set of chills to my skin. I can hardly get off the call fast enough.

Grabbing another glass of champagne to calm

my nerves, I fake smile my way through the sea of attendees in search of Amaryllis.

All eyes are on the podium as my father begins his dedication speech.

His voice is deep and steady, even though my extra senses are picking up on a strong undercurrent of nerves. "I'm pleased to see such a wonderful turnout. The men and women of the Duncan Restorative Justice Foundation will be circulating all evening to answer any questions you may have about how you can support and utilize our services."

Amaryllis leads a round of thunderous applause.

I pause and listen for a moment. I don't want my dad to see me grab his girlfriend and start whispering frantically in her ear. I'll wait until his focus shifts.

"Thank you. Thank you." Jacob pushes his palms toward the floor in an attempt to quiet the praise as his cheeks flush. "The real heroes tonight are the six former inmates who have chosen to commit to this program and be our guinea pigs."

One of the ex-cons, with a shaved head displaying a full-cranial tattoo, rubs his thick black beard and chuckles. "Better than labs rats, I s'pose."

The other five chuckle and my father shakes his head. "Sorry, guys. Public speaking isn't my thing. No matter what we call it, I'm grateful that you and your parole officers agreed to give this a fair shot."

The guys nod.

As Jacob turns to the group on stage and announces the names of the men who will be the first test subjects for his job placement program, I casually sidle up next to Amaryllis.

She takes one look at my face and gestures for me to follow her beyond the velvet ropes, upstairs to a private office.

When I walk into the room, the view of the stars twinkling above the vast great lake stretching across the harbor behind the building takes my breath away.

Amaryllis closes the door behind us, walks across the plush carpeting toward the large picture windows, and slowly turns to face me. Her features pinch with concern. "Is it bad?"

I swallow and nod. "It's pretty bad, but I don't think it has anything to do with Jacob."

As soon as she hears my father's not being investigated, her tense shoulders relax. "All right, give it to me straight."

"First, I'm obligated to say that this information doesn't leave this room."

She nods. "Goes without saying."

"The Pin Cherry Harbor Sheriff's Department

is working with the FBI to investigate an interstate gang of train robbers."

Her eyebrows arch comically. "Train robbers? Like bandanas covering their faces, six-shooters in the air train robbers?" Her hilarious pantomime of the hypothetical bandits makes me giggle.

Breathless from the laughter, I blurt, "I know, right?"

She regains control first and asks, "Seriously, what are you talking about?"

"Erick says it's a very small, highly efficient gang. They sound less *Butch Cassidy and the Sundance Kid* and more *Ocean's Eleven*. They've been working their way across the country robbing train cars filled with high-end electronics. Midwest Union is just their latest target. They're called the Stopwatch Robbers, because they never spend more than fifteen minutes per heist. He said the only predictable pattern is that they hit each rail line three times before they move on, but at completely unpredictable intervals. The first hit on Midwest Union went down last night. The search warrant is to check the train depot's employee records for new hires, and to examine the railcars on the siding for physical evidence. Erick claims they notified Dad's secretary."

Amaryllis drops her head like a rag doll, eventually looks at me, and rolls her eyes. "Hannah?

Hannah is barely a warm body filling a seat. I've told Jacob at least ten times to replace her. But she's a single mom with a young child and he somehow feels she deserves an eleventh chance."

I smile and my heart bubbles with warmth. My dad's a pretty good guy. The fact that he was responsible for one of the largest big-box store robberies in the history of Birch County is in the past. He served his time, paid his debt to society, and now he's paying it forward by helping others.

"Erick says that there's no suspicion on Dad, but they want to catch this gang before they move on."

"Thanks for making that phone call, Mitzy. I hope you don't think it was an abuse of our relationship."

My eyes fill with confusion. "Abuse? No way. I was looking for an excuse to snoop and your request gave me just what I needed to disobey Silas."

She laughs harder than I would've expected. "That man can be downright menacing. He was my professor for tort law, and even though it was more than a decade ago, the mere thought of drawing his displeased gaze during a lecture still makes me break out in cold sweats."

I join her laughter, but I'm a little distracted with this new piece of Silas's history that she drops into my lap. I had no idea he was ever a professor. Will wonders never cease?

Amaryllis opens the door and gestures for me to follow her. "We better get back downstairs before we're missed."

CHAPTER 3

THE GRAND EVENING eventually winds down, and by the time I drag myself across the alley to the bookshop, my feet are shot. I kick off the murderous heels and leave them where they lie, just inside the heavy metal side door.

The indignant wisp of my grandmother's ghost pops into view with an otherworldly moan. She wags a ring-ensconced finger at me. "I know ten women who would kill to wear those shoes for five minutes!"

"They can have 'em! My feet felt better after an eight-hour shift at the coffee shop back in Sedona." I push through her insubstantial mistiness and un-hook the chain at the bottom of the wrought-iron spiral staircase.

The thick carpets of the second floor Rare

Books Loft feel like heaven under my sore toes. I turn to lean on the banister and alternately stretch my calves as I inhale the enchanting scent of books.

The moonlight seeping through the rows of slumped-glass windows at the front fill my shop with a dusting of magic. The film-school dropout in me can easily picture a long, slow dolly shot that pushes in on a swirling mystery of—

"RE-OW!" Game on!

"Pyewacket! You scared the life out of me." My heart is racing and my breath is coming in short gasps. There's nothing quite like being lost in a spooky daydream, only to have a real live beasty leap at you out of nowhere.

The fright saps my last reserves. "Come on, you little terror. It's time for bed."

Leading the procession of human, ghost, and barely tame caracal, I reach up and pull the candle sconce that serves as the secret handle to open the sliding bookcase door to my gorgeous hidden apartment.

Grams simply vanishes through the wall ahead of me.

Swapping my designer gown for an old T-shirt, I collapse onto my eight-hundred-thread-count sheets and hit the button that closes my blackout shades. I don't want any over-eager sunshine ruining my sleep-in.

Unfortunately, my phantom roommate does not share my plans for ten to twelve hours of restorative sleep.

Grams keeps me up, begging for details about the soirée. As near as I can tell, the thing she misses most about being alive is high society.

"I would think you'd be just a tiny bit more interested in the train robbery, Grams." I'm tired and a little peeved by the lack of praise for my discovery.

She completely ignores my attempts to return the conversation to the clairvoyant message I received and my sleuthy call to Erick.

"What color did you say Amaryllis's suit was?" Grams clutches one of her many strands of pearls.

I exhale loudly with exhaustion. "For the last time, I think it was charcoal grey. Can't you just be pleased that I recognized it as a DKNY and let me get some sleep?"

"Oh, that would look lovely with her coloring." She floats closer to my large four-poster bed. "Was Jacob wearing—?"

"Reeeee-ow." The caracal's warning echoes through the shade-darkened apartment.

"See! Now you're even testing Pyewacket's patience." I throw a feather pillow at Ghost-ma.

She dematerializes before the pillow makes contact, and a haunting voice calls out from beyond, "Sleep is overrated!"

"Says the apparition," I retort.

A moment later she flickers back into view and her ethereal expression is laced with sorrow. "What I miss the most is being with people. Not that you aren't the most wonderful granddaughter in the whole world, but I miss the energy of a social gathering. I miss the compliments of eligible men . . . I'm sure you know what I mean."

I lie on my bed and stare up at the coffered ceiling. Do I know what she means? Men have always been more of a challenging distraction. I purposely keep my shattered heart locked away and leave men dangling at arm's length. But Erick is different. I think—

"Sorry to butt in, sweetie. It sounds like you need to talk."

"It's all right, Grams." Losing my mother before I even hit puberty meant that I never had any guidance in the romance department. It seems almost fitting that a sixty-something ghost that has chosen to look thirty-five will be my guide through the murky, ever-shifting landscape of love.

"I'll do my best, dear."

"Fair enough, but you can get out of my head now. I'll ask the questions of my choosing, not yours. Deal?"

"It's all a bit blurry, but I'll do my best."

That's as close to agreement as I'm going to get. "You once told me that you were happiest with Cal, when my dad was little. How did you know? I mean, what about how you used to feel about Odell? Do you wish you'd done things differently, now that you're dead?"

Ghost-ma shimmers uncomfortably. "Dead?"

Propping a few pillows behind my head, I settle in for a girls', or girl and ghost's, night. "Is that offensive? Should I call you life-challenged, or something?"

"Oh, Mitzy!" Grams giggles until she snorts. "I didn't mean it that way. I just don't 'feel' dead. I keep forgetting. It's not until someone like Twiggy or Jacob comes into the bookstore and completely ignores my greeting that I remember I'm not human."

"I'm sorry, Grams. If it's any consolation, I feel like you're still alive and I'm always forgetting that I'm the only one who can see and hear you."

She shrugs. "Well, except Pye. He seems to be on my frequency." She swirls closer and concentrates on giving her ethereal limb some heft while she pats my shoulder. "Now, about your relationship, let's talk about the birds and the bees."

I press a pillow over my own face and mumble, "Oh, brother! Let's not." Pulling the pillow back, I chew on my lip for a moment before I continue. "What I really want to know is how you know when it's more than just a fling. I mean, my mom clearly cared for Jacob. But they had a one-night stand, and even though she ended up pregnant, she never told him or tried to contact him again. I never understood that."

Grams floats up toward the ceiling. "There are so many levels of connection. When Odell came back from the war, we had an instant and powerful connection. My promise to wait for Cal evaporated in the face of that passion. If they hadn't fought so bitterly when Cal finally came home, I might never have turned to alcohol."

"Do you wish you'd stayed with Odell?"

"Sure, all the time. But it would've destroyed us." She sighs and drifts toward the scalloped-back chair by the coffee table. "Look what happened to my second husband, Max. We partied our way across Europe and our excesses ended up taking his life and one of my kidneys. Sure, that fateful accident was the thing that opened my eyes and motivated me to get help and get sober, but that could've been Odell."

"Maybe you would've gotten sober sooner for Odell." I shrug wistfully.

"That's the worst lie you can tell yourself. You can never use someone else as the excuse to get sober—or drunk. Taking responsibility for my actions was what allowed me to rebuild things with Cal. Those years we shared, raising Jacob, were some of my best."

"Do you think Erick is my 'Cal'?"

"Do you love him?"

My heartbeat suddenly thuds in my ears. The only person I ever loved was my mother. But now I'm building a wonderful relationship with my father and I love Ghost-ma so much it hurts.

Shimmering tears spring from her translucent eyes. "Oh, Mitzy. I love you too."

"Grams, you know I'm not comfortable with mushy stuff. I need to focus and figure out how I feel about Erick. I'm not sure if I'm ready to be exclusive, but I don't think I could stand to see him dating anyone else. Is that love?"

"It's a little jealous and possessive, but it's a start, sweetie."

"I've never felt like this before. I always push people away and act like a jerk before they get too attached. I don't want to push Erick away. Is that it?"

She kindly covers her smirk with her hand and offers gentle encouragement. "For you, it sounds like the beginning of something wonderful."

Pye slides his head under my hand and purrs noisily as I scratch between his tufted ears.

The rhythmic sound lulls me toward sleep and a massive yawn possesses my entire body. "I've got to get some sleep, Grams. I won't have the strength for proper snooping if I don't get a little shut-eye."

"Good night, my dear."

"Night."

CHAPTER 4

SPRING HAS FINALLY SPRUNG in almost-Canada, and I'm beyond ecstatic to have the opportunity to leave the bookshop in skinny jeans and a T-shirt, for the first time in months. I pull out one of my oldies but goodies for the occasion. The image on the front is a witch flying on a stir stick, above a bubbling cup of coffee, with the tagline, "Coffee is Magic."

Dutifully hooking the "No Admittance" chain behind when I reach the first floor is a matter of self-preservation. I should count myself lucky that Twiggy took a half-day off and wasn't waiting at the bottom, stomping her biker boots and yelling about my carelessness.

I almost break into song as I walk down Main Street toward Myrtle's Diner, basking in the late

May sunshine. I've nearly forgotten what it feels like to be warm.

The diner is unusually crowded, and I've come to understand this phenomenon as the first indication of some manner of festivities in town.

The short, grey, utilitarian buzz-cut of the diner's owner and chief cook, Odell Johnson, my grandmother's first husband, peeks through the orders-up window and he gives me a spatula salute.

I slip onto a red-vinyl-covered stool at the counter, and my favorite waitress, Tally, sets a cup of coffee down before I can pick up the newspaper.

"Good morning, honey." She smiles and nods, which causes her tightly wound, flame-red bun to bob back and forth. She's filled with a surprising amount of energy for a woman her age and clearly loves what she does.

"Good morning. How about all this sunshine?"

She grins, pokes a pencil through her topknot, and hurries off to refill mugs.

As a regular of the diner, I already know there's no need to place an order. Odell has his own sixth sense about what his regular patrons need, in the moment, and I can rest comfortably in the knowledge that my breakfast is already cooking.

Picking up the paper, I see no mention of a train robbery. Makes sense, I guess. Erick did say they were keeping the local investigation under wraps. Looks like I'll have to head down to the sheriff's station after breakfast if I want to get a real update.

Odell slides my plate of fluffy scrambled eggs with chorizo and a side of perfectly browned home fries onto the counter.

"Thank you, sir." I inhale deeply. This ritual, this touchstone of familiarity, soothes my soul. Routine is not something I found in the foster system. It has a wonderfully grounding effect.

He nods. "Sorry I couldn't make the shindig last night. The old deep fryer was acting up, and I had to sit around waitin' for the repair guy to show up. No good being without a fryer on opening weekend of walleye season."

And that would explain the influx of tourons—my clever compound word for tourist/morons—heavily scaled toward the male variety. The great lake, which spills into our harbor, is rumored to have some of the best walleye fishing up north.

"That's all right. It was just a bunch of stodgy old judges. The only interesting thing that happened all night, believe it or not, was when Deputy Paulsen came slinking in to get a signature on a search warrant."

"She accusing you of murder again?" Odell starts laughing before he can even finish the sentence.

And I playfully refuse to acknowledge his comment with a response. Not to mention, I can't share the details. "Anyway, everything went well. My dad's new venture is off to a great start. And I got to know Amaryllis a little better."

He smiles. "She's a good match for your dad. Always liked that girl." He raps his knuckles twice on the silver-flecked white Formica countertop and returns to the kitchen.

I gobble up my breakfast, as is my custom. I tried manners on for size for a hot minute, but food is delicious and best eaten before it gets cold.

I bus my dishes and slip them into the bin behind the counter as I nod to Odell. Waving to Tally, I head out toward my next stop.

The deputy I've nicknamed "Furious Monkeys" is manning the desk, and true to her moniker, she's busily tapping and swiping at her phone.

"So what level are you now?"

Without removing her eyes from her phone, she answers, "Finally hit 108." She nods over her shoulder, and I take that as my invitation to push through the slightly lopsided swinging wooden gate to Erick's office.

There's one deputy in the bullpen, busily typing at an actual typewriter! After all, this is the town that tech forgot. And things like credit card slidey machines at the dry cleaner, old-fashioned paper passbooks at the bank, and a majority of businesses that take cash only, are par for the course around here. I'm grinning with anticipation and my tummy is flip-flopping as I round the corner to Erick's office.

What the—

Imagine my utter shock and betrayal when I see him with his arms wrapped around some slutty brunette.

I gasp and cover my mouth with one hand, blinking ferociously to hold back the tears.

Erick's head jerks toward the sound and our eyes meet.

Unable to mask my hurt, I turn and rush out of the station.

Bursting into the bookshop, I ignore my volunteer employee's query and climb over the "No Admittance" chain hooked across the bottom of the wrought-iron spiral staircase which leads up to the Rare Books Loft. I thunder across the thick carpet and pull down the candle handle next to my recently recovered copy of *Saducismus Triumphatus*.

The bookcase slides open, and somehow I manage to contain my tears until it closes behind me.

"Sweetie, what's wrong? What happened?"

I throw myself facedown on the bed and sob

into my pillow until Pyewacket slinks across the duvet and lies comfortingly on my back. The reassuring warmth and weight bring an end to my self-pity, and I roll over and scratch him affectionately.

Grams swoops in to rub my shoulder with her ethereal hand. She's definitely gaining in her ability to take corporeal form, and, despite the fact that it's mostly weightless, the comforting intention hits home.

"This is everything I hate about lovesick nonsense! If I don't let myself care, then I never have to feel rotten."

"Ups and downs are part of life, dear. You just have to take things one day at a time."

"Argh! Grams, I seriously can't right now. All right?" I kick my legs, pound my fists into the mattress, and growl like a wild animal.

"My goodness. That's quite a little tantrum." She chuckles. "Looks like you may have inherited a penchant for drama from me. Sorry about that."

Throwing two more punches into a pillow, I exhale with a flourish and launch into my story. "I went down to the sheriff's station to see what I could find out about this gang, and instead of clues — I found Erick with his arms wrapped around some skanky brunette!"

"What?" Grams covers her mouth with a bejeweled hand. "Doesn't sound like Erick. He's such a decent guy. I can't imagine he would put himself in that situation. Seems beneath him."

"That's what I used to think. And you can see where it got me." I snuffle and wipe my nose with the back of my hand.

Grams shakes her head. "And you're always telling me that *I* could use a handkerchief!"

Her callback to our inside joke brings a momentary chuckle to my lips, but it's quickly replaced with another ladle full of self-pity. "I thought Erick really liked me. I guess he was just using me like every other guy in the history of ever."

"RE-OW!" Definitely sounds like Pye won't stand for this nonsense either.

"Exactly, Pyewacket. You couldn't be more right. Men, who needs 'em?"

Grams shrugs her designer-gown-clad shoulders and smooths her burgundy silk-and-tulle Marchesa. "I never did."

Fresh tears trickle from my shocked eyes. "Myrtle Isadora Johnson Linder Duncan Willamet Rogers, you can't be serious? Any woman with that many ex-husbands and an undisclosed number of special friends obviously needed something from men."

Uproarious laughter fills the apartment and

Grams feigns a spit take, which brings us another fit of giggles.

"There's plenty of fish in the sea, dear. Don't let one bad carp ruin it for you."

"I'm not sure any part of that analogy actually works. But I'll try to keep it in mind."

After splashing some cold water on my face and wiping away the mascara smudges under my eyes, I venture into the bookshop.

Down on the first floor, Twiggy is shelving a new haul of books from a huge estate sale in The Pines, the wealthy neighborhood in Pin Cherry, where the recent passing of an avid book collector was a real coup for our bookshop. Not to be too morbid.

Twiggy is in her mid-fifties and was Grams' best friend. She's one of the few living folks who knows about both my powers and my live-in ghost. She refuses to let me pay her for her efforts in the store. She claims to work for the entertainment, not the money.

"Any first editions?" I ask.

She nods. "Several. Mostly historical fiction, poetry, and a few biographies. I'll reach out to our list of collectors and see what I can unload."

"Thanks. And thanks for coming to my dad's grand opening last night. I know it's not your scene. Sorry I didn't get a chance to chat."

She clomps her biker boots down the stepladder and nods her grey pixie cut in my direction. "I can do without chit-chat. Anyway, figured I owed you one after you came to bingo with me, doll."

I laugh heartily as I recall my first trip to the local bingo hall. "Yeah, I guess that's not really my scene either."

"But you didn't disappoint. You managed to cause a commotion and get kicked out; just what I needed." She walks toward the back room, laughing uproariously.

And this would be the entertainment for which she works, that I mentioned earlier.

The remainder of the day finds me sulking on various pieces of furniture throughout the apartment, eating cold leftover pizza, and stealing several handfuls of Pyewacket's precious Fruity Puffs.

By nightfall my pity has turned into a slow-boiling rage over Erick's betrayal and I've decided I deserve a night out to drown my sorrows properly.

Grams pops into my *Sex and the City* meets *Confessions of a Shopaholic* closet and catches me slipping into a risqué diaphanous blouse and cami combination.

"Where are you headed?" Her voice carries a hint of suspicion and a soupçon of judgment.

"None of your snoopy ghost business." Unable to prevent the thought from materializing inside my head, I fall prey to her otherworldly thought-dropping.

Her eyes widen in shock. "Final Destination! You're going drinking?"

There's nothing quite like the indignation of a reformed alcoholic.

"First of all, we have a very clear policy against you eavesdropping on my private thoughts. If these lips aren't moving it's not fair game. And second of all, I'm not an alcoholic. I can enjoy a drink or two anytime I want. I respect your struggle, but I think what you're doing right now is called 'projecting.'"

"A drink or two! I recognize the mood you're in, Mizithra. I've been there too many times myself. And I know full well that you plan to go to that bar and drink yourself into oblivion. That's a dangerous side of town and a bar full of unscrupulous men. There's no reason to put yourself at risk, just because Erick Harper can't keep his hands to himself."

"That's where we disagree, Isadora." I throw on a stylish black leather jacket adorned with zippers and grommets, attempt to toss my short hair, and storm out of the apartment.

Grams pursues me all the way down the spiral staircase and over to the metal door leading to the alleyway between my building and my father's new headquarters, but her spirit is tethered to the bookshop.

I let the alleyway door slam and only feel a twinge of guilt over her muffled protests.

Backing my Jeep out of the garage, I drive directly to Final Destination, with the sole purpose of forgetting all about sheriff what's his name.

CHAPTER 5

THE SEEDY DIVE bar known as Final Destination is teeming with the dregs of humanity. And I say "known as" because the "s" is actually burned out on the neon sign. So it reads: "Final De_tination," which is probably far more accurate.

As I enter the questionable establishment I note that, evidently, fishermen enjoy their booze. Everyone must've caught their limit of walleye and they are celebrating in style. Avoiding several tables full of sweaty men who smell like bait, I take a seat at the bar and order a kamikaze. I throw out one of my favorite movie lines, "And keep 'em comin'."

The burly bartender with salt-and-pepper Travis Tritt hair stares at me for far longer than necessary, reminding me how young I must appear, and how recently I was exactly as flat broke as I look.

Slapping my ID on the sticky bar with one hand, I produce a wad of cash with the other. "Any questions?"

The barkeep smiles as though he's just landed the biggest fish in the pond and replies, "Not a one. Kamikazes. Rapid fire. You got it."

I'm pleased to see that we understand one another. I grab a bowl of stale bar mix and slide it across the peeling varnish to bring it into range.

Over the course of my kamikaze quest, two bar fights break out behind me. Both are quickly laid to rest by a large bat brandished threateningly by the solidly intimidating barman.

"I like the way you keep the peace, Dale. It is Dale, isn't it?"

He shakes his head. "You can call me whatever you want, Kamikaze Queen."

I raise my shot glass in a wobbly "cheers" to what's his name, throw it down the hatch, and tap it twice on the bar.

As the night wears on, various foolishly brave fishermen attempt to land Queen Kamikaze, but I set out with two clear intentions tonight: drown my sorrows and wake up in my own bed—alone.

It would've been smart to include a corollary about avoiding the pool tables, but I'm no psychic. Oh, wait, yes I am. Unfortunately, my extrasensory perceptions seem to go on the fritz when excess alcohol is consumed.

I head over to the tables.

The ingenious use of some cut two-by-fours levels the open table and its green felt has more than a few thin spots. A low-hanging light above the worn billiard arena displays a popular beer logo and casts a dim illumination on the motley crew assembled around the perimeter.

With a purposeful wiggle in my waddle, I rack the balls and hit a terrible break.

Tossing a stack of twenties on the rail, I throw down a challenge. "Best two out of three takes my money."

At least three guys queue up for the privilege. They Rochambeau for position with "paper" covering "rock" for the win, and I end up playing against a husky guy with a chin dimple who looks about thirty.

Doesn't matter. Joke's on him. I paid for the part of film school I actually completed with pool-shark money. "Put your money on the table."

He smirks at his buddies and obeys.

I lose the first game—of course.

He snickers as he hooks a thumb through his brown belt. "You picked the wrong game, girlie. Pool is a man's game."

I giggle and drunkenly rack the balls. Sure, I'm a little tipsy, but my act is what sells the grift. At least that's what foster sister number eight taught me.

He breaks and knocks in a solid. He misses his next shot.

I knock in a couple stripes and "miss" my third shot.

He hits three in a row, and I'll admit to a flash of anxiety.

When the play swings back to me, I clear the table and call the eight ball in the corner pocket.

His smug little grin fades and he racks the balls for game three in silence.

I chalk my stick real slow, blow off the blue dust, and break like a champ. Knocking in one of each, I ask, "What's your preference, slugger?"

His cheeks redden. "Solids," he mumbles.

"He called solids," I announce to the growing ring of spectators. I don't want him to suffer needlessly, so I wipe up the table in a nonstop flurry of cracking shots.

A smattering of applause comes from somewhere.

Before I knock in the final ball, I stop and lean on my stick. "Why don't you call the pocket, buddy?"

He looks at the eight ball and tries to imagine

the most difficult shot. The striped ten ball is blocking any direct shot at the eight ball, which hugs the far corner pocket. "Money ball, this pocket." He points to the hole right behind the ten-eight combo. "No combo shots."

I nod, chalk my stick and take aim. The tip of my cue smacks the white ball with sharp, angled force. The ball rockets forward with a low, but powerful loft. It lands firmly on the other side of my opponent's ten ball, cracks the eight, and sinks it in the corner like a basketball through a hoop. Luckily there was enough backspin on the cue ball to prevent it from following the eight into the pocket.

Cheers and hoots fill the bar.

He stands there with his male-chauvinist mouth hanging open.

Scooping up the cash, I smile and say, "I guess it is a *man's* game, son."

Admirers follow me to the bar, sidle up, and try to buy me drinks.

After several world-class smackdowns, I earn the nickname "Ice Queen," and the patrons leave a cautionary empty stool on either side of me.

The night is taking its toll, and I'm about to close out my tab, when I catch a very interesting conversation on my left.

"He says he'll mark the cars with the high-value

items. This is gonna be our biggest score. I can feel it."

"You sure we can trust this guy?"

"Totally. He did some time in Clearwater. Doesn't want to get his hands dirty, but we can buy his silence for two large."

"Chump change."

They clink mugs and down their beers.

In my current state of extreme inebriation, I shockingly opt to get out of Dodge with my tidbit of intel, rather than risk starting a third bar fight by interrogating these jerks.

I settle my bill with "Dale" and stagger out the front door.

An equally sloshed angler in the smoke pit makes one last desperate attempt as he sees me struggling to walk a straight line.

"You need a ride home, honey?"

"Not if your boat was the last one in the harbor, fish boy."

Don't worry, I leave my Jeep in the parking lot and stagger along the road toward the Bell, Book & Candle. I may not know when I've had enough to drink, but I definitely know when I've had too much to drive.

It's only a mile or two back to home base, and the cool spring breeze ruffling across the lake gives me a chance to sober up before I have to face the retribution of Ghost-ma.

By the time I reach the bookshop the evening's indulgence has caught up with me and I'm afraid my kamikazes aren't staying down without a fight.

CHAPTER 6

GRAMS CHOOSES to punish me for my indiscretion by abandoning me for the evening, but my stalwart companion Pyewacket is kind enough to lick my clammy face as I lie on the cool tile floor in the bathroom.

In the morning, I drag myself into the shower and wash the evening's bad choices down the drain.

Nothing fixes a hangover like french fries, so I make myself presentable before I leave for—let's call it—brunch.

Still no sign of Grams, so I make a general announcement to the four walls. "I thought you'd be proud that I came home alone. Not to mention that I overheard a juicy bit of gossip, but I guess you don't care." I push the plaster medallion above my mother-of-pearl inlaid intercom, and as the bookcase door slides open Ghost-ma rushes through the wall.

"I absolutely do not approve of what you did last night." Her crossed arms fall to her sides and she floats toward me. "But I still love you."

I hold up a finger to stop her advance. "And I don't approve of you abandoning me in my time of need." I tilt my head sharply for impact. "But I still love you, too."

And that's pretty much the longest fight Grams and I have ever had.

"Now what's this juicy gossip? Dish." Her shimmering eyes have an extra sparkle.

I knew she'd be unable to resist.

She opens her mouth to retort, but I point to my lips and shake my head before I launch into my tale. "There were a couple of guys sitting next to me at the bar discussing what I think was a train robbery."

"No way!"

"Yes way."

She hovers in front of me. "Are you going to tell Erick?"

"Not a chance." I cross my arms over my chest and frown. "Sheriff Harper is always quick to tell me how they solved plenty of cases before I came to town, so let's see how he does on this one without the helpful psychic messages and front-lines intel of Mitzy Moon."

"You can't go after these train robbers by your-self, Mitzy. That would be suicide. I won't stand for it."

"Simmer down, Annie Oakley. I have a better idea."

Grams rubs her bejeweled hands together eagerly. "Which is?"

"I'm going to go undercover as a bartender at Final Destination and see if I can pry some additional information from someone in the gang."

"Oh, Mitzy! This is your riskiest role ever." She swirls madly while she silently struggles with her decision. "If you promise not to put yourself in too much danger, I'll design the perfect wardrobe. I'm thinking redhead. What do you think?"

I always forget my grandmother was an amateur screenwriter. But I'm glad we're once again on the same team. "I'm not gonna dye my hair. I'm not that committed."

"Of course not. You should never dye that beautiful hair. I'm suggesting a wig."

"*Willie Wonka & the Chocolate Factory*! Are you about to tell me there's yet another hidden drawer in this place?"

Grams guffaws. "Follow me." She vanishes through the wall into my couture closet and my clairsentience picks up on her intense focus as she attempts to open one of two deep drawers at the bottom of the built-in stack.

"Here, let me help." I kneel and pull the drawer open to reveal a massive selection of wigs. There's every hair color imaginable, some natural, some not so much. A variety of lengths, cuts, and curls. Exactly what I need.

Grams is clapping eagerly and zipping around the closet in excitement.

Staring up at my swirling Ghost-ma, I have to ask. "Do I even want to know?"

She swoops to a sudden stop and her image flickers. "What? Can't a woman have a drawer of wigs?"

"Um, not usually. Were you a secret agent?" Thinking back, the only time I remember seeing so many wigs in one woman's possession was on the early 2000s series starring Jennifer Garner, *Alias*.

"Oh, I loved that show!"

Pointing to my unmoving lips, I scold her. "Grams!"

"My apologies, dear."

Gesturing toward the rainbow of wigs. "Are you going to explain, or would you like me to keep guessing? Because my next guess may slide toward the seedy side of theories."

She gasps in mock horror and plants a fist on her hip. "Mizithra!"

Shaking my head, I warn, "Truth clock's ticking . . ."

She floats toward the stash and I feel her energy shift as she struggles to focus and touch the assortment. "Mostly I loved to dress up." She runs her fingers through the silky tresses. "But there's some truth to the comparisons that Silas is always drawing between the two of us."

I lean forward eagerly.

"I was a bit of a snoop in my day." Her sparkling eyes dart toward me and she flashes her eyebrows playfully. "I met my fifth husband, Deacon Rogers, by posing as a chauffeur and holding one of those signs at the airport."

Leaning against a panel of built-in drawers, I giggle. "You didn't?"

"I did." She winks conspiratorially. "He was a famous, and devilishly handsome, author coming to town for a huge book-signing event. There were a gaggle of women staking out his hotel. I chose a more direct approach."

"But what about the actual driver? Did you knock him out or drug him?"

Clutching her pearls she cries, "Oh, Mitzy, nothing that daytime drama." She wiggles her shoulders. "I paid him off. You'd be surprised how cheaply one can purchase opportunities."

"You're dangerous!" Secretly, I have to admire her ingenuity.

"Thank you, sweetie. I thought it was quite clever."

All right. Not that much of a secret in the presence of a thought-dropping ghost.

"Sorry, dear. Snooping is a hard habit to break."

We both have a good laugh at that piece of honesty.

"Let's see what you look like as a sassy redhead!" Grams' eyes twinkle with gossamer mischief.

I pull out several variations on "red," arrange them on the padded mahogany bench in the middle of the closet, and prepare for my first "all wigs" fashion show.

Grams is clapping eagerly and zipping around the closet in excitement. After trying on each of the wigs two or three times, we decide the Reba McIntyre is too dated, and the Shirley Temple is too short.

The winner is a long strawberry-blonde—heavy on the strawberry—wig with soft curls.

My stomach growls loudly. "Listen, Grams, I've gotta grab some food before we take this any further."

"That's fine, dear. I'll come up with a name and a backstory. I'm sure if you offer to work for cash, that unscrupulous owner will hire you in a minute, without even asking for identification."

"Copy that." I lay the wig on the bench and head to brunch, filled with the excitement of a new case.

There's nothing like the thrill of a secret mission to make the sun seem a little brighter and put a spring in your step.

As my anticipation builds, I make a detour to the patisserie on Third Avenue, Bless Choux. I don't have time for a full breakfast paired with a casual perusal of the newspaper. Instead, I'm going to grab a coffee to go and a chocolate croissant.

Fortunately, the owner, Anne, is swamped. So, while she never lets her signature smile waver, she doesn't have time for folksy chit-chat today.

There's no chance to sink into the mouthwatering aromas and eye-catching displays. Patrons are queuing up like it's a blue-light special.

For those of you who missed out on those terrible "specials" at a certain low-end department store, let me offer a warning. There was never anything, under a blue light, or any other colored illumination, that was worth pennies on the dollar in that store.

The sea of humanity heaves me toward the pick-up end of the counter.

I grab my order, nod my thanks, and vamoose.

Sadly, my delectable pastry is gone before I make it back to First Avenue.

Luckily, I ordered two.

Now that my stomach is somewhat appeased, I can enjoy the sunshine and my second croissant with a touch more civility.

With a final grin at the sun, I duck back into my bookshop. Time to prepare to endure my secret-agent training and memorize my backstory. Whether I want to or not.

First things first.

Grams teaches me how to properly put on a wig and bobby pin it in place to avoid any unnecessary wig-slippage embarrassment.

I have to wonder if the only difference between drifting aimlessly through life and experiencing focused success is bobby pins. It would seem that each pivotal event since my arrival in town has been marked by the excessive use of bobby pins.

Regardless, I follow my grandmother's instructions.

"As you well should."

I narrow my gaze, but my system is flooded with far too much sugar to fixate on getting upset with Grams and her relentless mental wiretapping.

My standard skinny jeans will easily serve as proper attire for this character, who Grams and I have named "Daisy." Personally, I'm in love with the name because it reminds me of Daisy Duke waiting tables at the Boar's Nest. But Grams only agrees to the name because she feels it is suitably nonthreatening and won't draw any suspicion.

We argue over the appropriate shirt to finish off the outfit. I think it's worth showing a little cleavage, while Grams is pushing for something more demure.

"Look, this is a dive bar that caters to a primarily male audience. I'm going undercover to try to gather information. The last thing I want is for someone to recognize me and blow my cover."

"I am quite clear on the mission, Mitzy. What I don't understand is why you think dressing like a lady of the night will help you accomplish your task."

I slip on a black tank top with three snaps on a placket at the neckline. I rip open the snaps and squeeze my B-cups together.

The ghostly eyes of Isadora Duncan immediately dart toward my décolletage.

Smirking, I retort, "I think I made my point."

Her eyes flick up to my face and hover for a shocked moment, before she bursts into laughter. "I hate to say it, but you absolutely proved your point."

I dig around in the corner of the closet and pull out my ratty old denim jacket, a memory of my broke barista days, and prepare to put on the performance of a lifetime. "Wish me luck, Grams."

"Good luck, Daisy."

Laughing nervously, I head to the bus stop. With my Jeep still parked at Final D, it's not like I have another option. I could risk driving it home after my "interview," but if just one person sees me climbing into that Jeep, there's a chance they could make the connection between Daisy and Mitzy. And that's a chance I'm not willing to take. Plus, a broke vagrant willing to work for cash hardly seems the type to own a car.

CHAPTER 7

FINAL DESTINATION ISN'T MEANT to be seen in
the light of day. It's one of those establishments that
should only exist after dark. The dim neon sign,
with its uncooperative "s," warns you of what
awaits. The interior is illuminated as an af-
terthought, with darkly shaded wall sconces and
two long, low-hanging lights over the pool tables.

This isn't a place where people come to see or
be seen. They come to drink. They come to forget.
And those are exactly the things that I'm hoping
will work in my favor.

The front door creaks open against my weight
in a decidedly unwelcoming way and the filthy windows covered by moth-eaten brown curtains share
no secrets with the outside world.

A disembodied voice shouts, "We don't open until Happy Hour at four o'clock."

As I gaze around the dreary establishment, I wonder: How happy can it be? Oh, that's quite clever. I keep my amusement quiet.

While I gear up to introduce myself, I suddenly go off-script and decide Daisy has a southern accent. I gesture toward the faded help wanted sign in the window and slip into my best Texas drawl. "I'm here about this here job."

The large bartender, whom I previously nicknamed Dale, walks out from the back room and gives me a hasty once over. He crosses his thick arms over his barrel chest and his eyes linger on my cleavage.

It's impossible not to grin as I think about the "I told you so" I'll be giving Grams when I get home.

"That's an old sign. We're not really looking for anyone."

"I'm sure y'all could use some help. I can tend bar, clean tables, or just be your barback. I can even clean restrooms if you need me to. 'Cuz I just really could use the work." I tilt my head down and look up at him through my lashes.

He places his hands on the bar and clearly weighs his hatred of cleaning restrooms against his love of having no employees.

My extra senses whisper that he's weakening, so

I go for the close. "I'm no trouble at all. I work cheap. Cash under the table. Not a lick of trouble. Cross my heart." I brush my fingers in an "X" across my bosom and his eyes follow.

His face lights up and he takes a closer look at me. As he scans me over, top to bottom, his gaze lingers suspiciously on my face.

I let my red curls fall over my cheek as I look down at my shoes and utter a shy Southern belle giggle. "I bet I can sell more drinks than you tonight. Whaddya say? If I win, I get the job. If I lose, I mosey on down the road. Seems like a win-win for you, pardner."

The smile that curls his lip makes my stomach turn a little. "You got yourself a deal, babe. Only got the one register, though, so you keep track of your drinks on this notepad. We'll settle up after closing."

I'm not sure I like the sound of that. But it also seems like I might have a job. So, at this point, I pretty much have to agree. "Saddle up. You got yourself a deal." I approach the bar and put out my hand.

He reaches across with his huge mitt and engulfs my small hand. "Name's Lars. Welcome to Final Destination."

Not sure how I ended up calling him "Dale" the other night, but I'll need to make a mental correction ASAP. "I guess I'll see ya at four o'clock, Lars. Do I need a uniform?"

He snickers in a way that makes me feel like I need to take a shower. "What you got on is just fine, honey."

Gross. "Well, aren't you the sweetest thing."

I walk out of the roadhouse with a mixed bag of feelings. Yes, I'm rather pleased I landed the job. But I'm also extremely creeped out that I landed the job.

The skeevy chill on my skin dissipates as a perusal of the parking lot reveals my Jeep is no longer parked there. Stolen? Towed?

I check the bus schedule on my phone, and the next bus won't pass by for at least thirty minutes. I could walk over to the train depot and say hello to my dad, but I doubt he'll be very supportive of my undercover job. Maybe I'll give him a quick call and fish around in his pond of parking enforcement knowledge.

"Hey, Dad. What are you up to?"

He attempts a few pleasantries, but I can sense the tension in his voice.

"I won't keep you. I was just wondering if you know where the tow yard is in town?"

The fatherly chuckle that drifts through the phone does not amuse me.

"Why is that funny? Oh. You didn't— I mean, I could— Yes, it was thoughtful. Thanks. Bye."

Did you already guess? Dad saw the Jeep, all by its lonesome, when he drove into work this morning and he grabbed his extra key and took it back to the garage at the bookshop for me on his lunch hour. I feel simultaneously grateful and scolded.

Looks like I'll just wander back to the bookshop, enjoy the glorious weather, and bide my time until my shift starts.

Cut to me hopping off the bus at 3:45, bright and early for my four o'clock shift. If only my old supervisor from Hot Kafka back in Arizona could see me now! He'd be super proud of me, arriving early for my shift.

I walk through the door, take off my jacket, and stuff it behind the bar. If I want to have any chance of winning this "drinks" bet and securing employment at Final D, I need to know this place like the back of my hand.

Grabbing a rag, I wipe down the veneer and stagger the unappetizing bowls of stale bar mix at random intervals along the warped wooden surface. Checking the cooler to see what beers we carry, I make a note of the one bottle opener affixed to the pillar next to the register. We have an extremely limited selection of hard liquors, "well" brands or house pours only, and even fewer mixers.

There's no ice machine behind the bar, just a freezer filled with ice. I head down to the end of the bar and look for any possible clues that could lead me to the source of the frosty cubes. I'm about to open a door in the back corner when a gruff voice behind me shouts, "What d'you think you're doing?"

Deep breath. Texas twang engaged. I turn to greet my potential boss. "Howdy. Where d'ya keep the ice, Lars? I don't want to lose our little bet simply 'cuz I'm as lost as an armadillo on a highway." No idea about that saying. I'm pretty much making them up as I go.

A flash of recognition passes over his thick features. "It's Daisy, right? I didn't think you'd actually be back."

"What kinda lightning bug do you take me for? You and I made a wager, and I'm sure as sunshine not gonna miss a chance to show you up."

He makes a noise that sounds like a chuckle and proceeds to give me the nickel tour.

Two restrooms, a men's and a women's, but he assures me that the signs mean very little to the inebriated. There's a supply room, which contains the ice machine and a couple of white plastic five-gallon pails for transporting ice up to the cooler in the front. Any and all miscellaneous bar supplies reside in this room.

"We don't take credit cards. This is a cash-only bar."

Typical Pin Cherry business practice, and one less thing for me to learn. He shows me a change machine, by the two pool tables, which dispenses quarters for play.

"That about does it. You got any questions?"

"I reckon I'll know where to find you if I think of one."

The front door opens and two men are silhouetted against the golden late afternoon sun. They head straight back to a pool table and Lars pulls two long-neck bottles of beer from the fridge, pops the tops, strides across the watering hole, and sets them on the shelf next to the pool cue rack. As he walks back behind the bar, he nods in my direction. "That's two for me."

"Well, aren't you a long-tailed weasel. You've got me at a disadvantage, knowing your regulars like you do."

"Deals a deal," he says.

"No argument here."

I walk out from behind the bar, scoop up the bleach-soaked rag, and make my way over to one of the rickety tables posted up behind the billiards section. I bend way over as I studiously scrub the tabletops.

I hear some mumbling and a little snickering behind me.

Mission accomplished.

"Hey, fellas, today's my first day workin' at Final Destination. I sure could use a couple good ol' local boys who can help me get my bearings. Why don't y'all just let me know when you're fixin' to have another round? I'm your girl." Wink.

They both nod like well-trained puppies, and I can feel their eyes on me all the way back to the bar.

Lars shakes his head. "Now who's not playing fair?"

I innocently shrug my shoulders. "Love and war, right?"

The bar fills up quickly as the various workdays around town come to a close, and the fishermen come in from the lake. Fish tales abound. If their stories are to be believed, there can't possibly be any walleye left in the great lake.

I wiggle, smile, wink, and make more friendly conversation than I ever thought possible. The night wears on and I easily pull into the lead in the drinks competition.

The small handful of women who turn up at our establishment eye me with suspicion and resentment. This is clearly their territory and they're used to riding high on a lack of competition.

Lucky for them, I'm here for information and

nothing more. Unfortunately, the two men I'm most interested in seeing, don't turn up.

Looks like I'll be back tomorrow to pull another shift at Final D.

Currently, I'm absently wiping down the bar and keeping tabs on the drink levels of at least eight patrons. When I hear ice clink into the bottom of the drink in the booth next to the door, I quickly pour another rum and coke for plaid shirt, beer belly, blue hat.

Sliding his refill onto the table, I wink as I take his empty. Setting it on the bar, I check the clock. It's almost midnight. There's still a chance that my targets could enter before the 2:00 a.m. closing time.

The door creaks open as I head behind the bar to wash another sink full of glasses. When I look up to see if I can guess the drink order of our new customer, my throat constricts and I'm unable to swallow.

Sheriff Erick Harper just walked into my saloon. I put my head down and scrub dishes, hoping he's here to find some lowlife miscreant.

He wanders around the tables, passing out nods and friendly greetings, but my extra senses pick up on something more.

Attempting to shrink into myself, I double down on my glassware duties.

My mood ring turns icy on my left hand and I feel his presence without looking up.

Sheriff Too-Hot-To-Handle slides onto a barstool and places a photo on the drip rail. "Pardon me, miss. Have you seen—?"

I look up, glance at the photo on the bar, and subtly shake my head.

"Mitzy? Mitzy, why in the world—"

Continuing to shake my red curls, I stare daggers of warning at him.

"Hey, I don't know what you're up to, Moon. But we need to talk."

Lars walks out of the back room and looks from the sheriff to me, squares his shoulders, and narrows his gaze. "Sheriff, all our licenses are in order, and I don't need you giving my niece any trouble."

Here goes nothing. Leaning into the opening Lars offers with the "niece" comment, I take a deep breath. Texas twang engaged. "Hey, Sheriff, I'm Daisy. I don't rightly know who you're looking for, but you best believe you're barking up the wrong tree. You and I—we've got *no business* together." I add extra emphasis to the "no business" portion of my speech, in case he thinks I've forgiven or forgotten the trollop at the station.

Erick's face is a swirling mélange of confusion, hurt, and just a hint of amusement. "What are you playing at—?"

I don't know what possesses me, but there's no way I'm gonna let him say my name. My fist just comes out of nowhere and I slug him right across the jaw before I even realize what I've done.

As his head whips back and he falls off the stool, I attempt to justify the punch by shouting, "No means no, mister. I don't care if you've got a badge."

Lars steps up to the bar, pushes me behind him, and growls, "Get out of here before he stands up. See you tomorrow night. You're hired."

Grabbing my jacket from under the bar, I hightail it toward the back door that I thankfully noted during my tour.

I don't have time to figure out bus schedules, so I take off at a brisk pace toward home. The damp night air is cooler than I remember from my previous night's hike, but that could have something to do with the fogginess of that inebriated memory.

The hasty pace of my retreat keeps me warm and I'm only about a block from the Bell, Book & Candle when a siren briefly chirps and red and blue lights swirl down the alleyway as the patrol car turns in front of me.

Sighing, I shuffle down the alley after the cruiser, ready to face the inevitable. I lift both of my hands in the air before Erick even exits the car.

He steps out of the vehicle, rubs his hand across

his jaw, and shakes his head. "Give me one good reason not to slap the cuffs on you, Moon."

My accent and all pretenses evaporate. I'm upset and he's gonna hear about it. "I'll give you two. First: You're in no position to take the moral high ground, and B: Technically, you were harassing me."

He shakes his head. "You can put your hands down. And about that moral high ground, I don't know what you think you saw at the station—"

"Look, I've been on my feet for hours and I've got another shift to work tomorrow night. Let's just leave it at 'I don't really care what I saw,' and I'll see you around."

He attempts to lighten the mood. "What happened to that southern accent, Daisy?"

"I guess it disappeared along with common decency, *Sheriff*."

The metal door opposite mine opens into the alley and my concerned father steps out. "Everything all right, Sheriff?"

Erick lets out an exasperated sigh and shakes his head. "Maybe you can talk some sense into your daughter, Jacob."

My dad shields his eyes against the swirling lights and squints. "What the heck did you do to your hair, Mitzy?"

Great. As if Erick hadn't already ruined my

night enough, now I'm going to have this conversation with my dad. "Why don't we continue this discussion inside, Dad?"

He tugs his robe closed and tilts his head as he takes in my attire. "Should I be concerned?"

Before I can answer, Erick steps toward me and lowers his voice. "Will you at least let me buy you breakfast in the morning and explain?"

"I can't be seen in public with you, Erick. I can't risk blowing my cover."

Jacob is close enough to hear my last few words and chuckles. "The joys of parenthood, eh?"

Erick runs a nervous hand through his thick blond hair and a section of his slicked back bangs falls across his face.

The sexy image is almost more than I can resist.

He somehow senses my weakness.

"How about I pick up a selection of your favorites from that bakery on Third and bring breakfast to you?"

The desperation in his voice melts my last bit of resistance. But I'm not going to let him know. "It's a patisserie, and the *pain au chocolat* is amazing. I'm agreeing to eat pastry in your vicinity—nothing more."

"10-4." Erick lets a small grin sneak onto his face as he climbs back into his cruiser.

Jacob puts an arm around my shoulders and chuckles. "What's new, Red?"

Once inside the back room, I yank out my bobby pins, whip off my wig, and scratch the be-jeezus out of my scalp. "I have a whole new respect for actresses."

My dad raises an eyebrow. "Okay."

"It's just that it's difficult to act all sweet and flirty when your head itches like a sack of fleas on a hound dog." Apparently, "Daisy" left a little character residue.

Jacob gestures to the wig. "Are you gonna tell me, or do we have to play twenty questions?"

I chuckle. "Right. Let me make us some hot chocolate and I'll tell you my tale." In the movies, when families have late-night discussions there's always cocoa. Of course, I only have packets of instant, but there are tiny marshmallows, which would make a nice close up for the B-roll.

Setting a mug in front of my dad, I plunk myself down in the chair opposite him. "Wow, it's been a while since I spent an entire shift on my feet. I'm happy to say that being an heiress seems to agree with me far more than toiling away at a minimum wage job."

My dad grins. "Let me get the ball rolling. I think I heard Erick call you Daisy. Is that right?"

The heat rises on my cheeks and I take a long,

slow sip of my hot chocolate before I reply. "Promise you'll hear me out before you make a decision."

Jacob gives me a two-finger salute, "Scout's honor."

"So, I'm working undercover at Final Destination." I stop and wait for his stream of objections.

He mockingly locks his lips with an invisible key and tosses the key into the middle of the table.

I shake my head. He definitely gets his sassiness from Grams.

"You're back! I was so worried. How did it go?"

Speak of the devil. Luckily, a part of me was expecting this otherworldly pop-in and prevents any late-night pants accidents.

However, my out-of-the-loop father's arms bristle with goosebumps and his eyes dart from side to side. "Is it Mom? Is Isadora here?"

Since I've always been able to see and hear my grandmother, I forget that not everyone can. And it seems like those folks who can't communicate with her always get the ghost-chills when she appears. "Yes, Grams is here. Now I only need to tell my story once." I take another drink of my hot chocolate before I explain the reasons for the undercover gig, for my dad's benefit. Then I bring everyone up to speed on the events of my first shift.

A dark cloud passes over my father's face. "It

sounds like Erick might've deserved the right hook, but I'm far more concerned about you hunting down a dangerous interstate gang."

Silence hangs over us, and Grams is so still it's almost as though someone freeze-framed her.

My dad leans forward and grabs my right hand. "You should get some ice on those knuckles. But where did you learn to hit like that?" He shakes his head. "He actually hit the ground?"

If I didn't know better, I'd say there's a hint of pride in my father's tone. I won't spoil the moment by pointing out that Erick was precariously balanced on a barstool at the time, and that I sucker punched him. Those details seem insignificant in the face of this precious father-daughter moment. "One of my foster brothers was an undesirable. He taught me how to fight, and pick locks and pockets."

Jacob releases my hand and retrieves a bag of frozen peas from the freezer. He lays the bag across my knuckles and returns to his seat.

His features are pinched with guilt, and I'm not sure how to break the uncomfortable silence.

"God grant us the wisdom. That's all we can ask for." Grams attempts to pat Jacob on the back, but he jumps in his chair and a fresh set of shivers shake his shoulders.

"Tell him what I said, Mitzy."

Right. I keep forgetting I'm an afterlife interpreter. "Grams is spouting her Alcoholics Anonymous aphorisms. But in this case, I'd have to agree. You didn't know what I was going through back then, Dad. You didn't know what had—happened—to Mom. The past is the past. Everything that we went through got us to this moment."

His shoulders relax a fraction of an inch and he reaches out to adjust the bag of frozen veg on my hand. "Thanks for giving me a chance to be part of your life. Please don't take that away from me by getting yourself into some kind of irreversible trouble."

"You mean by punching Erick? He absolutely deserved it! I don't know what he takes me for, but I don't appreciate being made a fool of."

"Regardless of your personal relationship with him, Mitzy, he is the sheriff. You should exercise a little caution."

Shrugging off my father's advice like a real daughter, I scrape my chair back from the table. "I need to get some sleep. I'm beat, and I've gotta work another shift tomorrow."

Jacob rinses out our mugs and tosses the peas back in the freezer. He slips one arm around my shoulder and gives me a squeeze. "G'night, Daisy."

I follow him to the side door and wave as he crosses the alley. I throw on an extra-heavy twang for his benefit. "G'night, Pa!"

His shoulders shake with laughter as he disappears into the building next door.

It's comforting to have him nearby. When winter comes and the temperatures drop below freezing, I may reconsider his suggestion about joining our buildings with an enclosed skywalk, like Frida Kahlo and Diego Rivera.

Turning, I walk straight through Grams. "Geez! Give a girl some warning."

Glimmering ethereal tears trickle down Ghostma's cheeks.

"What's wrong?"

She snuffles and fiddles with one of her pearl necklaces. "I miss being alive. There's a big part of me that wishes Jacob and I could've reconciled while I was still on this earth—as a human."

"Everything happens for a reason, right Grams?"

She nods, but if my ghost-radar is as accurate as my human-based clairsentience—she's having some trouble accepting the things she cannot change.

CHAPTER 8

DESPITE THE FACT that Erick and I are feuding, I can't stop my heart from racing when I think about sharing breakfast with him. And with the absence of cold winter nights, it doesn't seem all that practical to entertain guests in my reindeer onesie. But I'm not about to appear desperate enough to don full hair and makeup for breakfast.

A quick trip to the closet lands me a comfortable pair of super-soft leggings and a nice, casual, oversized boyfriend sweater.

Not that I think of Erick as a boyfriend—especially not after his shenanigans at the station. That just happens to be the proper name for the garment. Which I, of course, learned from otherworldly fashion consultant, Grams.

"What are you going to do about your hair, dear?"

I'm about to retort with a very snarky "nothing," when I gaze at my reflection. "Uffda." I learned that local expression of dismay shortly after I arrived in town, and, I have to admit, I kinda love it.

The good news is that my hair has finally grown out from the cross between the Cardi B pixie and a Betty White curl-bob that graced my noggin when I arrived in Pin Cherry. The bad news is, I haven't had a haircut in months. Images of *The Shaggy D.A.* come to mind.

In my bathroom, I slide open the drawer on my left and grab a pair of scissors.

Snip. Snip. Slash. Snip. Slash. Snip. Snip.

"What on earth?" Grams covers her mouth with both glimmering hands and gasps.

I scoop up the pile of hair, throw it in the trash bin, and *shake my head darling*. Jose Eber would be so proud. "It's just one of the many skills I learned while I was financially challenged."

She chuckles, but nods her approval. "You're actually pretty talented. You probably could've made a heckuva lot more money cutting hair than making coffee."

I nod, but hold up an admonishing finger. "You're forgetting something."

She lifts her phantom limbs as she shrugs. "What's that, dear?"

"Cosmetology school would've cost money. Money that I sadly did not possess at the time. And now it seems—"

BING. BONG. BING.

The three gongs, signaling an arrival at the alley door, jumpstart me into action.

Grams swirls around me gleefully. "He's here, sweetie."

I tug the edges of my sweater as I mock curtsy and use my best Daisy voice. "I declare. I have a gentleman caller."

Grams ghost squeals and I wipe laughter tears from the corners of my eyes as I hurry across the Rare Books Loft.

Stopping for a moment, I attempt to catch my breath before I open the door. "Hey."

Erick lowers his head and offers up his bright pink bakery box as a peace offering.

I snatch the box and let the door slam shut.

Before he even has a chance to ring the bell again, I push the door open and chuckle. "Kidding. Just kidding. Come on into my swanky back room and I'll make you a crappy cup of coffee."

The look of shocked amusement on his face would make a delicious meme. Maybe something like, "When she takes your pastries, but not your apology."

He quietly follows me inside.

My extra senses pick up on Erick's nervousness and I'm already dreading everything he has to say. Looks like I'm about to hear how another one got away. Why are the good ones always taken?

I busy myself boiling water, adjusting the single-pour on top of a mug, and measuring out the coffee with the Twiggy-approved scoop.

He fails to take a seat at the table. Instead, he paces the small space. For a specimen his size, that is barely two strides in either direction. It's a bit like being trapped on a hamster wheel with a ferret, and it's driving me insane.

"Erick, please sit down and have a pastry."

He nods and sits half on/half off the chair. Also, he does not open the box and select a breakfast option.

I place his cup of coffee on the table, but he doesn't pick it up.

Exhaling with annoyance, I say, "Erick, drink your coffee."

"I'll just wait for you." He smiles awkwardly.

I want to yell and scream and tell him to drink his coffee when it's hot. But what does it really matter? It's his coffee. If he wants to drink it lukewarm that's his business. I finish making my cup and take a seat at the table. For the record, I take a sip of my hot coffee—while it's hot.

He makes no move to open the pastry box, and I'm not one to be shy about food.

Flipping open the lid, I grab a chocolate croissant and take a massive bite, staring directly into his dreamy blue-grey eyes as I chew.

Erick leans back under the weight of my stare. "I wish you would've given me a chance to explain at the station."

"Oh, is that what you wish. Well, I wish I hadn't walked in on you making out with that woman. That and a quarter will buy me a whole sack of nothing." Something I learned a long time ago is that wishes are for the fortunate. My mood ring tingles lightly on my left hand, and I glance down in time to see a small stuffed teddy bear. The hairs on the back of my neck stand on end, and I have growing concerns that his information dump is going to get worse before it gets better.

He shifts in his chair. "I know this is going to sound like a line, but it's not what you think."

I shove another bite of chocolate croissant in my mouth, cross my arms over my chest, and scoff. A light puff of crumbs escapes my mouth along with the sound of my disbelief, and I feel embarrassed rather than superior. Struggling to control my facial expression, I barely hold onto my glare.

"Karen and I served together in Afghanistan."

Great. How can I possibly be angry once he pulls the military service card? Clearly, I can't. So now I'm forced to release a fraction of my disdain and attempt to listen dispassionately. "And?"

"And we were briefly involved." He avoids eye contact and rubs one thumbnail with his other thumb.

I roll my eyes. "Picking up where you left off then?"

"Not exactly." He grows very still and his voice is barely a whisper when he continues. "She married my best friend in the unit and they both reenlisted."

My arms slowly uncross and fall to my sides of their own accord. A wave of guilt washes over me. "That must've been hard for you."

"Not as hard as what happened next." He wrings his hands and I watch his Adam's apple as he struggles to swallow the emotion.

"What happened?" My own throat tightens as I anticipate the dark turn this story will take.

"Turns out my buddy came back pretty messed up and started drinking a little to ease the pain. Eventually, it turned into a lot of drinking and some unacceptable spousal abuse."

All of my anger and jealousy vanishes. "I'm so sorry, Erick. I had no idea."

He shakes his head and shrugs. "Neither did I. Karen just told me everything yesterday."

"Oh. That's the worst."

"I wish that was the worst."

I lean forward and reach my hand across the table toward him. To my surprise, he slips his hand in mine and squeezes my fingers hard. "They had a son. When he hit the kid, she packed up her stuff and left him." He rubs his thumb across my fingers. "The custody battle got pretty ugly, and four days ago he kidnapped the boy and disappeared from South Carolina."

Well, I am a complete heel, and no doubt deserve every drop of karma I'm about to receive. "And she came to you for help?"

"Denny said he had relatives in Pin Cherry. That's why we always hung out together. We'd talk about fishing and stuff to keep ourselves sane during deployment. He mentioned something to Karen about a cousin having a cabin up here somewhere, when they were still together. She thinks maybe he's hiding out there. I'm looking into land records to see if I can find it, but there are a lot of lakes and a lot of cabins around Pin Cherry. Sometimes land is handed down for generations, and plenty of cabins are built without permits. So I told her I'd do what I can, but it's a needle in a haystack."

I squeeze his hand and look warmly into his

concerned face. "I'm sorry I jumped to conclusions, Erick. You didn't deserve that. I have to stop assuming you're like other guys." I don't mention how rotten I feel for calling Karen a skank, but I only said that to a ghost, so I think I'm forgiven. "You're not like other guys. Apparently, you're a saint."

Our shared chuckle breaks the tension and I turn the delectable box of pastries toward him. "I thought you said we were having breakfast *together*."

He nods and grabs a large jelly-filled doughnut.

I can't contain my laughter.

"What?"

"Like I always say, a lot of stereotypes are based in truth." I point to the doughnut, point to his badge, and shrug.

He manages to laugh without choking on his mouthful of pastry and we exchange understanding smiles over a moment of silence. "If there's anything I can do, any way I can help you or Karen, let me know. Even if it's just to throw money at the problem. Whatever you need, Erick. I'm here for you."

His jaw clenches with emotion and he nods.

My clairsentience picks up on a wave of relief and gratitude. I feel like I'm not playing fair, but it's not as though I can turn my psychic senses off at will.

Erick takes a swig of his cold coffee and fixes me

with a very stern gaze. "Now, would you like to tell me what Daisy's doing working at Final Destination?"

I'm forced to reveal my undercover investigation into the interstate train robberies, and I'm surprised when Erick doesn't jump on the disapproval bandwagon and chew me out.

"What would you say to making it official?"

My heart races and my cheeks redden. Is he about to ask me to go steady? Wow! From our first couple's fight to making it official in one breakfast. This is moving fast, even for me. "It seems kind of fast."

The look of confusion that washes over his face tells me all I need to know about my misinterpretation of his words.

"I mean, what do you mean?" My cheeks must be flashing neon red by now.

A flicker of understanding passes through his eyes and he hastens to change the subject. "I could really use a CI on this case. Would you be willing to come down to the station and sign some papers?"

And there's the rest of the story. He would like me to be an official CI, a confidential informant. Not an official girlfriend, not a steady girlfriend, not a main squeeze. A confidential informant. I'd like to be indignant, but after so recently getting my pride handed to me in a humble pie, I decide to accept his offer. "The only way you're gonna get me down to the station, copper, is if you haul me in and charge me with assaulting an officer."

He drops my hand and leans back. "Boy, oh boy, I'd say you're brilliant if you weren't so diabolical."

I cross my arms and grin smugly. "My shift starts at four. You know where to find me."

He stands, tips his chin down in that way that implies a hat being doffed, and shakes his head as he leaves.

CHAPTER 9

THE RELIABLE BUS drops me at the corner across from Final Destination right on schedule. I appear to be making a habit of arriving early for work.

Lars looks up as the door creaks open. "Daisy, I wasn't sure you'd be back."

For a split second I forget what a southern accent sounds like, and a momentary panic grips my chest. The aphasia passes and I fall into character. "Now, y'all know I won that bet last night. And bringing the cops in here to chase me off ain't gonna get you out of payin' up."

He chuckles as he stacks some clean glasses on the counter. "The deal was you got a job. Seems to me I already paid up."

"Fair enough, darlin'. How can I lend a hand?"

"Why don't you wipe down the tables and run this little broom around the floor. It's been a while."

I keep my overwhelming agreement to myself and get busy turning this sow's ear into a silk purse. Well, "silk" is a stretch. It's more like a flaming bag of dog poo, and I'm just trying to put out the fire without getting anything on me. I suppose that's certainly not something Daisy would say, but between you and me, Daisy's a little bit of a goody-two-shoes.

Every time the door opens my mouth goes dry. At some point, Erick is going to show up and I'll have to put on one heck of a performance. Maybe he'll change his mind, and he'll get a break in the case without using a CI.

As the place fills up, the drink orders are coming in fast and furious. I am overwhelmed with my real waitress duties and forget to be on guard.

Heading into the supply room, I fill two five-gallon pails with ice and walk down to the end of the bar to refill the cooler. As I set my buckets down, the hairs on the back of my neck, my real hairs, not the wiggy ones, stand on end. There's something about the two guys at the end of the bar that seems vaguely familiar. I dump the ice cubes and rush back into the supply room.

I need a quiet place to practice one of Silas's lessons. He always told me that my extra senses pick up far more than the regular ones. And he did teach me how to replay a memory with psychic enhancement. So here goes nothing.

Thinking back to the night in the bar when I was drowning my sorrows, I recall the snippet of conversation that caught my attention. I replay the phrases slowly in my mind and let my extra feeling, knowing, hearing, and seeing take center stage.

The timbre of the men's voices is crystal clear.

One man has short black hair and a scar on his left cheek.

The other man has shoulder-length brown hair pulled into a ponytail, and a barbell piercing through his right eyebrow.

I feel their smugness. They genuinely believe they are above the law. Untouchable.

As I take note of the neck tattoos on the short-haired man, the supply closet opens and I squeal in fright.

"Sorry, doll, thought it was the bathroom."

Instead of turning to leave, though, the misguided drunk continues to stagger toward me.

Time for Mitzy to take the lead. I spin him firmly around and shove him out the door. I'm about to give him a very unladylike piece of my mind when Lars walks around the corner. "This guy bothering you?"

Daisy fans herself with one hand as she replies.

"He scared me near to death. I was puttin' the pails back in the supply room, and he just barged right in. My heart is still all a flutter."

Lars puts a strong hand on the man's neck and steers him toward the front door. "Time for you to go."

Walking behind the bar, I paste on my southern-fried grin and pretend to wipe down the bottles across from my suspected train robbers.

They don't seem to be all that chatty, but from what I can tell the remarks they are making tend to be about my backside.

"Now now, boys, that ain't no way to talk about a lady."

Ponytail leans forward with his tongue hanging out. "Oh, that accent is just what I needed."

His friend snickers suggestively. "Why don't you come around this bar and let me get a better look at you." He winks and pats his lap.

"Tell you what, why don't I make y'all s'more drinks instead?"

"Now, that's a woman after my own heart." Ponytail punches his buddy on the arm.

I mix a seven and seven and swirl the ice around until it's nice and cold. Then I pretend to trip as I try to set the glass on the bar, and spill the ice-cold drink right in his crotch.

I won't repeat his extremely rude stream of expletives.

"Oh dear, I am so sorry." I throw a filthy rag in his direction. "Makin' another drink right away, darlin'."

He continues to unnecessarily slander my person.

But before I can make a replacement drink the front door opens and the moment I *haven't* been waiting for all night is on.

Erick looks at me for a second, and then pretends to search the room.

Bless Lars and his giant heart. He sidles right up to Erick and clearly tries to talk him out of taking me in.

The sheriff looks around the owner's broad shoulders and I dart my eyes to the left, hoping he picks up my signal about the possible gang members.

He pats Lars on the shoulder and walks straight behind the bar. He's staring right at me. Erick puts one hand on his gun and stops a good ten paces from me. "Daisy, I'm gonna ask you to put your hands on the bar and stand very still."

Ponytail and his buddy slide off their stools and melt into the crowd. Clearly, they do not want this sheriff to notice them.

Erick takes out his cuffs. He pulls my wrists behind my back and prepares to slap me in irons, as he lists off my Miranda rights.

Wow. You've got to give him bonus points for authenticity. Looks like it's time for me to put on a show.

I yank my right hand free before he has time to lock that cuff, and I take another swing at him.

He's faster and stronger than I imagine and he snags my loose arm, bends it behind my back, and locks the handcuffs down before I have a chance to utter a word.

Would it be wrong for me to say it's a little bit of a turn on?

"Looks like we'll be adding attempted assault, to your assault charge, Daisy. Let's go."

Lars shakes his head as Erick leads me out of the bar.

I smile at my boss as I drag my feet toward the exit. "Don't you worry, darlin'. I'll be back for my shift tomorrow night."

I jerk my shoulders and attempt to pull my hands free.

Several of the patrons applaud my resistance.

Out at the cruiser, Erick gives me the classic hand-on-head tuck into the back seat and slams the car door.

He drives out of the parking lot and whistles. "I can't believe you took another swing at me!"

Dropping my character's accent, I reply as Mitzy. "I had to play the role, right?"

He shakes his head. "A little too well."

As we turn onto First Avenue, I panic. "You're not taking me back to the bookshop are you?"

"Where else would I take you?"

"You have to take me to the station and book me. Call it in on the radio, or whatever. We've taken it this far, Erick. I have to make sure Lars and the rest of the Final D crowd think I'm a legitimate reprobate."

"It's not that much of a stretch."

I roll my eyes. "Ha ha."

"Fine, we'll run it by the book. You want me to ask Deputy Baird to call Silas and have him meet us at the station?"

I exhale in frustration. "I think you should see if there's a public defender."

Now it's Erick's turn to scoff. "Look, Daisy, this cover story and your disguise aren't going to hold up to actual scrutiny. If I call in a public defender, we'll be worse off than if I'd taken you back to the book-shop. Let's just head into the station, sign the CI paperwork, and you'll be on your way."

I don't like Erick's lack of commitment to my plan. I chew on the inside of my cheek and replay scenes from fifty movies in my mind. "I've got it!

Get the judge to appoint Silas as my assigned counsel."

The snicker from the driver's seat lets me know that my idea, while amusing, has merit. Erick places a call on his cell phone and, from what I can hear, the judge seems eager to do anything that could aid in the arrest of this train-robbing gang.

As soon as we park in front of the station, I prepare to put on another performance.

Sheriff Harper beats me to the punch. "Come on, Daisy." He pulls me out of the cruiser and steers me, a little roughly, through the front door and past the swinging wooden gate. "We'll put you in a holding cell until your counsel arrives."

My bravado wanes in the face of hanging out with other lowlifes in a jail cell.

As Erick locks the bars behind me he whispers, "Lucky for you it's a slow night. You've got the place all to yourself."

"Silas is on his way, right?"

He shrugs noncommittally and the outer door clangs behind him.

I plunk my felonious behind on the cold metal bench and immediately regret my latest scheme.

CHAPTER 10

AFTER AN ENDLESS LECTURE FROM SILAS, covering everything from unnecessary risks to unnecessary assaults of local sheriffs, he finally runs out of steam. With a final harrumph into his bushy grey mustache, he bails me out.

However, his indignation does not stop after I sign the CI papers and we leave the station. He continues to mumble disappointed admonishments under his breath as he walks me back to the bookshop.

We both stop in front of the ornate front door, exchanging confused glances.

Silas exhales. "I assumed you were aware that you possess the only key to this door, Mizithra."

Fantastic. My misbehavior has landed us in

formal first-name territory. "I'm not sure if you re-member the size of that heavy, triangle-barreled brass key, but I usually keep it on a chain around my neck." I point to my unusually low neckline. "There's not re-ally a place to hide that kind of jewelry in this outfit."

He once again harrumphs into his mustache and knocks on the beautiful, but thick, wooden door.

"Also, the key to the alley door is in my jacket pocket, back at the bar. Don't you have a key to the side door?" I ask.

"Not since the break-in, when the door was rekeyed."

"Oh, sorry. I'll make sure Twiggy gets you a copy." I join him in banging on the door, in hopes that Grams will hear us and be able to muster enough energy to turn the tumblers. The days may be warmer when the sun's up, but the wind whistling across that great lake in the blackness of the wee hours is sending quite a shiver up my un-der-dressed spine.

"Mitzy, is that you?"

"Grams! Hooray! Do you think you can open this door?"

"Shoot. I've been writing my memoir for the last few hours and I'm not sure how much I've got left in the tank."

I relay her message to Silas and his already droopy shoulders sag further.

He places a hand on the door and offers his encouragement. "It's no rush, Isadora. Take your time. Gather your strength."

Arching an eyebrow, I chime in, "Speak for yourself. You're wearing that thick tweed blazer, and I'm standing here in a tank top, because Sheriff Harper didn't have the decency to grab my jacket when he arrested me."

I hear Grams gasp through the door. "Arrested? Arrested?"

"Don't worry about it. It's all part of the plan. You just focus on opening this door." I lean my back against the brick entryway and slide down to the sidewalk. I may not have worked my full shift, but my feet are still sore from the previous day. I can't believe how quickly I've lost my endurance.

Silas drapes his blazer over my knees and bare arms.

"Thanks. You didn't have to—"

"A gentleman never *has* to; he chooses chivalry."

And now we wait for ghostly grandmother to "recharge."

My finger aimlessly traces along the carvings on the beautiful door. A centaur chasing a maiden through delicate woodland. A faun playing a flute for a family of rabbits dancing around his cloven feet. The shadow of a winged horse passing in front of the moon. A wildcat stalking a small boy. As my touch falls on the fiendish feline illuminated by the streetlamp, I remember what I wanted to ask. "Silas, why does this carving look so much like Pyewacket?"

Silas groans as he bends to follow my finger and, when he sees the cat in the carving, he chuckles until his cheeks redden and his loose jowls jiggle.

My head tilts to the side and I chew the inside of my cheek. "I'll give you a minute to enjoy your private joke, but then you're going to tell me the story behind this door."

He presses a hand against the bricks and straightens. "I found this door in a quaint little reclamation shop in San Miguel de Allende, Mexico. The proprietor informed me it had been imported some years before, to a local private collection, and displayed inside an artist's casita on the property. The collector had recently passed and this gentleman had scooped up most of the items. Paintings, sculptures, chandeliers, and several hand-carved doors. We eventually agreed on a price, and he shipped the door to Pin Cherry Harbor. It was—"

"It was a gift for my grand opening! Isn't it divine?"

The end of Silas's story is lost in my grandmother's outburst. "Grams ruined the ending of your story. So, now I know where the door came from, but why does this cat look so much like Pye? It even looks like there are the same scratches over the left eye?"

Silas nods and smooths his grey mustache with his thumb and forefinger. "I believe it's commonly known as a 'chicken or egg' paradox."

I shake my head and sigh. "I guess it's not all *that* common, because I have no idea what you're talking about."

Silas leans down, reaches into the pocket of the jacket draped over my lap, and removes his pipe.

I'm fascinated. I've always smelled the pipe smoke on and about his person, but I've never actually seen him smoke a pipe. Momentous.

"A 'chicken or egg' paradox is one in which it is impossible to discern which came first." He tamps the tobacco in the bowl, strikes a wooden match against the brick, and makes a "pwahp, pwahp, pwahp" sound as he pulls the flame into the bowl of the pipe to ignite the tobacco. It's mesmerizing.

Smiling as I soak in the experience, I nod. "All right. I accept your definition. What does that have to do with the door?"

He exhales a puff of smoke that smells of cherry and vanilla. "The question is, did the carving on the door exist before Pyewacket, or did Pye exist before the carving?"

"Grams said she won him in an off-the-books Scrabble game, so that had to be after she got this door. Right?"

Silas tucks the pipe into the corner of his mouth and wags his head back and forth in a way that neither agrees nor disagrees. "Perhaps."

The last tumbler clicks into place and Grams cheers. "I did it!"

Getting to my feet, I give an exhausted exhale. "You did it. Thanks, Grams." I turn toward Silas, hand him his blazer, and offer my thanks. "I appreciate you bailing me out. Now that everything's official, we shouldn't have any more complications."

He grips the thick bowl of the pipe with his right hand. "That hardly relieves you of the responsibility of keeping me informed."

"Copy that. But, I've got to get some sleep before my next shift, or I may be too tired to be Daisy."

A final cloud of smoke lingers in the doorway as Silas toddles off toward his 1908 Model T parked on Main Street near the sheriff's station.

I enter the bookshop and lock the door behind me.

Grams is all questions, and I'm all out of patience. I blurt out a couple of facts and command her to leave me be until my alarm goes off.

Stumbling up the stairs, I collapse onto my empty bed, fully clothed, just like the good ol' days.

I'm sure Pye will join me before dawn.

My alarm goes off at 1:00 that afternoon and frightens me half to death. I flail wildly until I get a hold of the phone and silence the interruption. I wish I felt rested, but my dead-to-the-world, dreamless sleep barely seems to have recharged my batteries. I lie back on my pillow and stretch my arm out to scratch Pyewacket's head.

The spot beside me is still empty.

"Grams! Grams, where are you?"

She snaps into existence right in front of my face and I jump backward. "Easy! I'm barely awake, and I haven't had a single cup of liquid alert."

"It sounded urgent, dear. I came as quickly as I could."

"Have you seen Pyewacket?"

She circles slowly toward the ceiling. "Let me see. I know I saw him yesterday afternoon. Little devil snatched a sheet of paper from my writings and I chased him up and down the stairs of the museum."

Grams always has been partial to the third floor

displays in the museum. It's where she first learned to hold a quill pen in her ethereal hand, and wrote me a message I will never forget. "I love you, Mitzy."

"And I still do, sweetie. But I'm concerned about Pyewacket. Maybe he's trapped in the museum."

Something doesn't feel right, and my stomach suddenly swirls with nausea. I race out of the apartment, past the carefully aligned rows of oak tables, each with their own green-glass reading lamp, down the spiral staircase, through the bookstore, and into the museum.

"Pye? Pyewacket, where are you?" There's no sign of him. And in the short time I've lived in this building, I've never known him to be trapped anywhere. He clearly has his own set of secret passages, or maybe even secret powers, and being a victim isn't one of them.

"Any sign of him, Mitzy?"

"Nothing." Worry creases my brow. "Grams, you check the high places in the bookshelves on the balcony, and I'll search the museum top to bottom."

"Understood." She salutes me with her bejeweled hand and passes through the wall, back into the bookstore.

I stand very still next to our Gutenberg printing press display and reach out with all my senses, regular and extra, to see if I can possibly feel my fur baby's energy.

Just as an icy tingle twists through my mood ring, I hear hacking and coughing that sounds like something trying to work up a furball.

"Pyewacket!" I run up the stairs to the second floor and find my poor kitten wedged under an old eighteenth-century copying press.

"Come here, baby. It's okay. It's just a furball. Go ahead and cough it up. Don't worry about it. No judgment."

Pyewacket continues to hack and choke.

Hunkering down, I aim my phone's light toward my beasty. A closer look reveals gunk in the corners of his eyes and a trickle of blood running down his sweet chin.

Dear Lord baby Jesus! Something's really wrong. I race down three flights of stairs, into the bookstore, and back toward the apartment—nearly tripping over Twiggy.

"What's the rush, doll?"

"Something's wrong with Pyewacket. He's coughing up blood." Emotions are overwhelming me and I can barely keep back the tears. I run into the apartment and grab a towel. By the time I'm rushing back across the bookshop, Twiggy yells after me, "I rang the vet. Doc Ledo's nurse said to bring him in right away. They'll clear out a room."

Twiggy may be a little rough around the edges, but she's always there for me when it matters most.

Scooping Pyewacket up, I wrap him in the towel. The fact that he offers absolutely no resistance is a testament to his dire straits.

Hopping into the Jeep, I break every traffic law between me and Gunnison Avenue. Swerving into the parking lot, I jump out of the car with Pyewacket in my arms. I don't even take time to shut my door. I just run inside the clinic with this adorable, irritating creature lying limp in my arms.

The nurse takes one look at me and waves us straight into a room.

Doc Ledo wheels through the opposite door and nods reassuringly before he starts shouting instructions.

I can barely choke out my concerns before the tears overwhelm me. When did I become this much of a softy? How can I possibly love such an aloof animal this much?

Doc Ledo hands me a box of tissues. "Don't worry, Mitzy. Nothing's going to happen to Pyewacket on my watch."

I nod and blow my nose.

He scoops Pyewacket into his lap and rolls his wheelchair into the back.

Time seems to almost stop. It feels like days have passed and no information has come back through that door. I'll never forgive myself if something happens to that cat. He took a bullet for me and my dad, and if I can't manage to keep him alive, maybe I don't deserve to own such a special creature.

When the door opens and the doctor returns empty-handed my heart breaks.

He wheels over and puts a gentle hand on my shoulder. "It's all right, Mitzy. Pyewacket will be okay. He somehow swallowed a nasty bit of plastic, and it got lodged in his throat. The MRI showed me everything I needed to know, but I had to sedate him to extract the foreign object."

I press a hand to my churning gut. "But he's all right? He's alive?"

Ledo chuckles and puts a finger under my chin. He tips my head up and adopts a fatherly tone as he says, "You and I both know that cat has at least six lives left."

Happy tears spring from my eyes. "When can I take him home?"

"It will take a few hours for the sedative to wear off, and I wouldn't mind keeping him overnight to make sure there weren't any serious lacerations to his windpipe."

"Can I see him?"

He nods. "Of course. Follow me." Opening the

rear door to the exam room, he leads me back to the surgery suite.

The sight of Pyewacket so absolutely still and seemingly lifeless nearly brings a fresh set of tears to my eyes. But the slow, reassuring rise and fall of his chest lets me know he's alive.

My magicked mood ring zaps my finger with an unwelcome heat. A quick glance at the dome of glass reveals Pyewacket coughing and spitting up blood.

Thanks, ring. That's an image I definitely want to see again. Not.

The hairs on the back of my neck tingle and I manage to unravel the clue. "Doc, you said he choked on a piece of plastic. Can I see it?"

He wheels over to a small stainless-steel table and lifts a piece of that classic blue fabric. His hand disappears for a moment and returns with a nasty twist of red plastic. He reaches across Pyewacket's quiet form and drops it into my palm.

Turning it over in my hand, I look for any indication of its origin. "Where do you think he got this?"

Doc Ledo shakes his head. "I don't recognize it. When I first saw the MRI, I thought possibly it was part of a bottle cap, but the plastic is thicker, more rigid."

"Do you mind if I keep this?"

He shrugs. "Be my guest."

"Thanks for seeing us so quickly. I definitely owe you one."

He smiles and leaves to see his other patients.

As I sit next to Pyewacket and scratch between his black tufted ears, I think back to the first story I heard about the doc—before we even met. A classic Pin Cherry moment if ever there was one.

I couldn't keep Tally straight from Tilly, and good ol' Twiggy was trying to clear up my confusion, in her no-nonsense way.

"Tally works at the diner. Tilly works at the bank. They're sisters. Folks say their parents named each of the kids after the town where he or she was conceived. Now I'm not saying it's an appropriate system, but the oldest sister got made in Tillamook, Wisconsin, and goes by Tilly. The youngest got made in Tallahassee, Florida, and goes by Tally, and the brother in the middle got cooked up in Toledo, Ohio, and goes by—"

"Toley," I had blurted.

Of course, Twiggy was having none of my interruption. "What the heck kinda name is Toley? No, wise-acre, he goes by Ledo," she said.

And the rest, as they say, is history.

CHAPTER 11

WHEN I RETURN to the bookshop it's dark, and I'm emotionally and physically exhausted. I stumble upstairs, fall into bed, and I'm pretty sure I'm asleep before my head hits the pillow.

Waking sometime later, shivering and confused, I grab my phone to check the time.

How can it be 2:00 a.m.?

My internal clock is all messed up, and I haven't eaten since—ever. I head straight downstairs and into the back room to microwave absolutely *anything*.

While my leftover Chinese food spins on the turntable, I gobble down a few handfuls of Fruity Puffs. My tears flow freely when there's no warning cry from Pyewacket.

PING.

The second the microwave beeps, Grams is all over me.

"What happened? How's Mr. Cuddlekins? Where is he? Why isn't he with you?"

I aim an imaginary remote control at her and shout over her queries, "Does this thing have 'pause' or maybe 'mute'?"

She comically freeze-frames, and we both laugh louder than necessary.

As the tension dissipates, I'm able to bring Grams up to speed on Pye's accident and prognosis.

"Plastic? What kind of plastic?" She taps her hand on her chin as she thinks.

I reach into my pocket and recover the deadly chunk of red. "This." I drop it into her outstretched hand and it lands on the floor with a thud.

Our eyes meet and we cackle like crazy women.

Before I can come up with a snappy commentary, my phone rings.

"It's Silas." I put the call on speaker and Grams starts babbling again.

"He can't hear you, Grams."

Silas waits a beat. "Good evening, Mitzy. How was your shift?"

"*Mystic Pizza!*"

Grams and I exchange a horrified glance.

"Silas, I'll call you back in a minute. I've got to

call Lars." I hang up on Silas and call Final Destination.

Turns out, Lars is surprised I'm already out of jail and he wasn't really expecting me to show up tonight.

Cool. Saves me having to come up with a weird lie. Daisy says, "Thanks, darlin'. I'll see you tomorrow at 4:00."

Grams wipes her flawless brow with a dramatic gesture and grins. "That was close."

"Was it? It actually seems like reliability isn't expected from transient barmaids who work for cash."

BING. BONG. BING.

I shrink into my skin and whisper, "Who could that be?"

Grams nods her concern. "And at this hour."

I tiptoe to the metal door facing the alley and, in my gruffest voice, ask, "Who is it?"

The sexy chuckle is all I need to hear.

I'm already opening the door as he replies, "Erick."

"Well, aren't you a sight for sore eyes."

He grins and steps inside. "That was very 'Daisy' of you. How was your shift? Did you get any intel?"

What is it with everyone suddenly being so interested in my "shift?" I bring Erick up to speed on

Pyewacket and my preoccupation at the veterinary clinic.

"So, you didn't go to Final D?"

"I thought I just explained the situation with Pyewacket? Of course I didn't go to my fake job when my fur baby was clinging to life."

He smiles in that warm, sexy way that makes my insides melt.

"What?" I shrug.

"You're a softy. You act tough, but you love that cat as much as your grandmother did."

I hear a sniffle behind me. "Isn't he the sweetest thing?"

Thank heaven for telepathic ghost communication. *Grams, if you don't suck it up and leave me in peace, I will personally find a way to confine you to the apartment!*

"Mitzy?" Erick leans his face dangerously close. "Are you in there?"

I jump self-consciously and step back. "Sorry, it was just when you mentioned my grandmother—it almost felt like she was here for a minute." I attempt to cover the snark in that comment with a wistful grin. "But that's crazy, right?"

Erick leans against the wall and quietly ponders my question. "Not that crazy. I've heard a lot of stories about people getting messages from the other side. In fact, I've had a few locals claim they sensed a presence at your grandmother's memorial service —right here in this bookstore. I know it sounds weird, but I think there's more to the afterlife than dirt naps."

I'll avoid his reference to Grams with a ten-foot pole, but based on what I know about his time in the Army and the friends he lost over there, I get where he's coming from. "It's comforting to think that they might be able to hear our positive thoughts, you know?"

He nods, and his eyes get that faraway look that's always a mix of pain and honor. "Yeah, it is."

I plunk myself into a chair and power through the rest of my sweet and sour chicken while Erick brings me up to speed on the progress, or lack thereof, the task force is making.

"The FBI guys are so focused on the 'new hires' angle. Unfortunately, the two guys that recently took jobs at the depot are both from your dad's program. Then there's a guy he placed down at the docks . . . They don't want to follow any other leads. They're like a dog with a bone. I need to clear these ex-cons, so the Feds can move on to something more useful. I have one more name to clear. The guy I was looking for when I came into the bar the other night, Anthony Jenkins. I need to find him and get his alibi. Maybe I'm wrong, but I think there's something we're missing."

"Don't worry, I'll get you a real lead. Now that I'm a wanted criminal, they'll welcome me with open arms."

He nods slowly and reaches up to rub his gorgeously stubbled chin with his right hand. "Oh, is that why you hit me? I thought it had something to do with the whole 'Karen' misunderstanding."

I blush in what I hope is an adorable way and not a guilty-as-charged way. "It might have been a little bit of both. I'm sorry if I hurt you."

His hands drop to his lap and he stares down as he rubs one thumb with the other. "Same."

Grams was right. He is the sweetest thing. "Life is a learning curve, right?"

He sighs and suddenly looks up with a sparkle in his eye. "Hey, where did you get that right hook, though?"

"Oh, you can thank my foster brother Jarrell for that. He was an incredibly bad seed, and apparently saw real potential in me. He taught me a few basic cons. Including the 'lost puppy tearjerker.' And he showed me how to fight so that I'd have his back when we got caught in someone else's territory."

"Wow, just when you think you know a girl. I had no idea you were such a scrappy juvenile delinquent. Maybe I should see if I can get a copy of those records from Arizona."

My face goes as white as my hair and I lean forward. "Those records are sealed. You can't—"

"Easy, Patty Hearst. I was only kidding. But I gotta say, that reaction makes me awful curious."

"I think it's time to call it a night, Sheriff. I need a good night's sleep if you want me to give a convincing performance tomorrow; I mean, this afternoon." I stand and toss my empty take-out box into the trash.

Erick pushes his chair back and my psychic senses pick up on his hesitation and his thinly veiled desire.

For some reason I'm not ready for this next step, so I rush past him and hold the alley door open. "I'll call you on my way home tomorrow night; or actually, tonight, since it's already tomorrow. Thanks for checking on me, Erick."

He brushes past me, and my tummy flip-flops.

As he steps out into the dark alley, he looks back over his shoulder. "Hey, I really do hope Pyewacket is all right. It's pretty special to have a link like that to Isadora. She'd be proud of the way you take care of him."

Oh sure, pull at my heartstrings when I'm trying to resist melting into your arms, Erick Harper. Stay strong, Mitzy, stay strong. "Thanks, I'll see ya 'round." I hastily pull the door shut and lean against it as I pant.

"See you around." Did I really just say that? Get it together, Moon. I set the alarm and hurry upstairs to the apartment.

As I snuggle into my comfy bed, I'm struggling to balance my emotions. I can't decide how to proceed with Erick. The old me, party-girl me, would've easily entertained a one-night stand and ruined any chance of something more meaningful. This new, work-in-progress version of me wants to take things slow and explore the possibility of a grown-up relationship with, like, goals and stuff.

I swear I hear a ghostly snicker somewhere in the ether.

I roll over, punch my pillow a few times, and pray to the dream goddess for a special episode of my mental mini-series: "Erick Harper: Dreamboat."

CHAPTER 12

Sadly the deities of dreamland failed to deliver my special request, and when the ringing of my phone rudely awakens me, I feel neither rested nor happy.

However, my mood rapidly improves when Doc Ledo tells me Pyewacket is more than ready to be picked up. I hope my fiendish feline won't mind if I make a quick stop at Myrtle's Diner. I haven't had a real breakfast in days, and I miss Odell's curmudgeonly face.

My classy outfit consists of skinny jeans, canvas high tops, and a hoodie that says, "Coffee this good should be illegal," with a picture of a coffee cup handcuffed to a patron.

I clomp down the iron circular staircase and

somehow manage to keep from falling, even though my tired leg catches on the "No Admittance" chain.

"I thought I heard your thunderous approach, Your Highness." Twiggy cackles at her own joke.

"When's the next reading day, up in the loft?" Since inheriting the bookshop, I've learned that my grandmother made a habit of opening the Rare Books Loft to researchers once per month. Twiggy takes the appointments, some which come months in advance, and sets up each station with the requested book and white gloves. It's all very hoity-toity.

"Not till next week." She hooks a thumb through the belt loop of her dungarees and narrows her gaze. "Since when have you been interested in the actual running of this place?"

"Touché." I acknowledge her retort with a bow. "I just want to make sure I'm here to get a real good look at everyone. Part of me still worries about that snake in the grass, Rory Bombay; that he'll somehow try to sneak back into my life, or, worse, my bookshop."

Twiggy pounds her right fist into her left palm. "Let him try."

That's new. Her actually defending me? Today must be my lucky day. As I remember I'm about to pick up Pyewacket, I double down on my grin.

"You look pretty pleased with yourself, doll. Where're you off to?"

"The most delicious breakfast in town, and then I get to pick up Pye from the vet."

She breathes an audible sigh of relief. "That cat sure knows how to get himself into trouble."

"Seems like he takes after Grams more than any of us realized."

Twiggy's eyes widen before she doubles over with a huge belly laugh. "He's not the only one," she manages to gasp out between guffaws as she waves her finger at me.

"Rude." She's not wrong, though. "I'll see you around, after I pick up Pyewacket."

Her only response is continued laughter.

I'm happy to report that the folks at the diner are very pleased to see me and don't feel the need to make jokes at my expense. Although Odell is asking a lot of questions about where I've been the last few days and how many meals I may or may not have missed. If I didn't know better, I'd say he's a tad jealous that I may have been dining out on him.

"Hey, Tally, your brother did me a solid. Pyewacket swallowed a nasty piece of plastic and he definitely would've choked to death if Toledo hadn't performed an emergency surgery."

Tally bobs her head up and down in agreement, and her tight, flame-red bun follows suit. She refills my coffee as she replies, "It's almost like Ledo's accident never happened. He's got that whole clinic converted for easy access from his wheelchair, and he tells me business has never been better. You know I'll never be able to repay you for finding the person that ran him down, but I hope you won't get tired of letting me try."

I smile up at her and raise my mug in a toast. "To the best coffee in Pin Cherry."

She blushes, but nods appreciatively.

After a delicious swig of go-go juice, I add, "Besides, I'm pretty sure I'm the one getting the better end of this deal. Free burgers and fries for life and hot coffee at the ready . . . What more could a girl ask for?"

The scrape of Odell's spatula comes to a sudden halt and he peers through the red-Formica-trimmed orders-up window. "I guess the girl might ask for another date with the local sheriff, if she was smart."

Looks like I spoke too soon. Apparently, today I get to be the butt of everyone's jokes. "I'm turning over a new leaf, Odell. I'm going to take a page from Isadora's handbook and let Sheriff Too-Hot-To-Handle pursue me."

I am mildly offended by the volume of laughter this prompts. Even sweet ol' Tally is forced to cover her mouth to hide her snicker.

"You know what? I have a very important person to pick up from the animal hospital. I don't need to sit around here and be abused by the likes of you two."

We all share a laugh, and I absolutely finish my liquid alert before I take my leave.

My heart is thumping with excitement to see my little guy, and my foot may or may not rest heavily on the accelerator.

The moment I walk through the front door the nurse is on me like white on rice.

"Mitzy! Thank goodness. Pyewacket is beside himself. His caterwauling is driving the dogs insane. Follow me." She hustles me into the back, and as soon as the door opens I hear my spoiled little boy making his needs known.

I stop several strides shy of his enclosure. "Robin Pyewacket Goodfellow, I insist that you calm yourself this instant. We're going straight home, and if you don't behave yourself there will be no Fruity Puffs for you."

The instant silence is deafening.

The nurse looks at me as though I'm some sort of witch doctor.

Between you and me, I feel a little bit like I channeled Dr. Doolittle just now, but we won't tell her.

I stride over to Pyewacket's cage, crouch, and

open his door a crack. "And you promise you'll be-have and walk straight to the car?"

"Reow." Can confirm.

"Then we have an accord." I open the door the rest of the way and he haughtily saunters out.

He casts an evil glare at the nurse, swishes his tail, and marches directly to the door.

As I open it to leave, an odd whisper drifts to-ward me. "I never would've believed it if I hadn't seen it with my own eyes. You're like some kind of Cat Whisperer."

Let her think what she likes. "Please thank the doc for me. I'll get this guy out of your hair. Thanks again, to everyone."

Pyewacket figure eights through my legs before leading the way out of the clinic. He walks directly to the Jeep and waits patiently for me to open the front door. He jumps in and sits in the passenger seat like he thinks he's people.

However, he refuses to allow me to put the seat-belt around him, so I drive back to the bookshop with the utmost caution and at a speed that brings to mind scenes from *Driving Miss Daisy*. Which makes me giggle uncontrollably like a loner maniac, when I think about the fact that, technically, I *am* Daisy.

Grams and Twiggy descend on us the second we enter through the alley door.

Twiggy has a freshly poured bowl of Fruity Puffs for his royal furriness, and Grams ghost-cuddles the crap out of him.

But the second he buries his face in his food bowl every human and ghost takes a large step/swirl back.

Speaking from experience, one does not pet Mr. Cuddlekins when he is consuming his sacred children's cereal.

After he finishes his snack and his ablutions, he fixes me with a knowing stare. "Ree-ooooow."

This intonation is new, and it sounds to me like a query.

"Is this about the plastic?"

"Reow." Can confirm.

"I have no idea what it means, but I know you well enough to know that you don't do anything by accident. So if you're asking if I kept it, I did."

He appears to nod his head in a very human way before he bounds through the bookshop and leaps to the top of the stacks. Two turns around in a circle and he collapses into a heap of tan fur.

Before I can "poor baby" him, Grams beats me to the punch.

"Poor baby. He was probably up all night in those substandard accommodations."

"Oh brother." I squeeze my eyelids closed.

She instantly turns on me. "Don't you 'oh

brother' me, young lady. Mr. Cuddlekins was at death's door. He deserved eight-hundred-thread-count sheets and a golden chalice filled with Fruity Puffs. They probably gave him tap water. Tap water! The thought of it."

I roll my eyes and attempt to keep my thoughts to myself.

Time for me to get serious about making it to my shift at four o'clock. I need a really good outfit and a much better push-up bra. Time is running out, and I have to get to the bottom of the looming heist.

Just as I dive into my closet to search for a wardrobe upgrade, my phone pings with a text from Erick.

"Can you meet me and Karen at Myrtle's?"

I text back. "I accepted your apology. No meeting needed." Plus, no need to mention how much I'm so not in the mood to meet Karen.

PING.

He doesn't take "no" for an answer. Instead he tries flattery. "She read about you in the paper and wants your help finding her kid."

Well, if I refuse now I'll look like a real "B." My fingers tap out a reply. "Has to be now. Has to be quick. Need time to 'Daisy' before I catch the 3:30 bus."

PING.

"We'll order you some fries ;) "

I find "Daisy's" look for tonight, toss the wig on the pile, and hustle downstairs.

When I walk into the diner, Odell is eyeballing me with concern over a tub of plates and empty glasses, and Erick is waving foolishly, as though he's not the only guy sitting in the now-empty diner.

As I approach the booth, I paste on a smile.

Erick stands and fumbles a handshake. "So, um, Mitzy Moon, this is Karen Garcia-Jordan. Karen . . . Mitzy." He slides into the booth on Karen's side of the table.

I nod politely, but ignore her outstretched hand. Yes, it is childish, but I haven't decided how I feel about this chick yet.

Before I can sample a golden fry or say a word, my ring turns to ice and I glance down to see the worried face of a little boy. All right, universe! I'll stop pouting.

"Thank you so much for meeting us, Mitzy." Her perfect full lips smile warmly.

"Of course." However, between you and me, I'm not crazy about the way she said "us," like Erick and her are together. Oh boy! I'm having some real issues getting my *issues* under control.

"I was reading about some of the cases you've solved since you came to Pin Cherry and I'm—"

Her voice catches and she pauses to wipe her tears and blow her nose.

It takes every ounce of my sorely lacking self-control to ignore Erick's comforting arm around her shoulders. Her dark hair is pulled into a messy ponytail and the bags under her rich-brown eyes indicate a severe lack of sleep. A wave of unconditional love and heart-stopping fear wash over me from her side of the table, and I finally release my misgivings as I feel a mother's terror for her lost child. Blinking back my own tears, I offer my help. "Do you have a picture of your son, or your ex-husband?"

She sniffles and digs through her purse for her phone. "This is Breck. He's six."

I take the phone and look at the photo. I'm not surprised to see that it's the boy from my ring's message. He has his mother's olive-brown skin and warm smile.

She takes it back, swipes through a few images, and hands it to me. "And this is Denny."

As I touch the phone, I see a different image in my mind. It's of this man on her phone, but with facial hair and a broken nose. "Is this recent? Does he have any facial hair or maybe injuries?"

Karen gasps and looks at Erick. "That's uncanny."

Erick shrugs. "What? What's uncanny?"

"That picture is only about six months old. But Denny did grow a beard and mustache since then, and his nose got busted in a bar fight just a couple weeks before he took Breck."

Erick stares across the table and tilts his head to the side. "That *is* uncanny."

I slide her phone back across the table. "We can all stop saying 'uncanny.' I'm just being thorough."

Erick chews the inside of his cheek and stares suspiciously. "That's one word for it."

"It was nice to meet you, Karen. I've got to get to my— to work. I'll keep an eye out for Denny and let you know if I come up with any leads."

Her hand shoots across the table and she clutches my arm with a death grip. "I don't have a lot of money, but I'll give you every cent if you can save my little Breck."

Having just faced losing Pyewacket, I can more than imagine how much she must be hurting. "You don't have to worry about money. I promise, I'll do everything in my power to find Breck." There's no need for me to mention that my powers may extend beyond the realm of normal.

"I'll be in touch." I slide out of the booth and walk toward the door.

Erick catches up to me and grabs my hand tenderly. "Thanks, Moon. It means a lot."

I lean close enough to crowd the Holy Ghost

and whisper, "I'll think of a way for you to repay me."

He blushes.

I wink and swagger out of the diner. Smirking to myself I whisper, "Still got it."

CHAPTER 13

FRIENDS ARE FAST AND SHALLOW in the dive-bar scene, but Lars is all smiles when I make my grand entrance from the 3:45 bus drop-off.

"I was gonna call my bondsman if I didn't see you today," he jokes.

Daisy nods and smiles warmly. "That's right thoughtful of you. Luckily, I'm what you call a 'small-time crook.' Seems like that sheriff has bigger fish to fry."

Lars chuckles and dumps two buckets of ice into the cooler. "I heard somebody caught a walleye that broke the record today. Things could get crazy tonight. But after that punch you threw, I guess you can handle yourself in a fight." He smiles admiringly.

I give a clumsy curtsy. "That I can. That I can."

Lars definitely knows his people. By ten o'clock the roadhouse is packed, and I'm pouring drinks and popping caps off beer bottles faster than I ever thought I could. Although, it's hard to be a spy and a good waitress at the same time.

Despite my high hopes for the evening, the two men I had pegged as members of the train robbery gang never show. And with the decibels pumped out by the rambunctious crowd, it's darn near impossible for me to eavesdrop on anything.

My phone buzzes in my back pocket and I duck into the supply room to check it.

"Meet me out back in five."

It's a text from Erick. Odd, since I don't have anything to tell him. Looks like I'll have to take up fake smoking to go along with my fake accent and my fake job. I deliver a tray of beers to the rowdy booth in the corner and endure the second slap on my backside of the evening.

Lars catches my eye and nods. He storms toward the table to have a word with the handsy patrons and I bum a cigarette off him as he passes. "Thanks. I'm just gonna step out back real quick."

"No problem. I'll take care of these guys."

I snag an abandoned lighter off the bar and slip out the back door.

No sign of Erick. Looks like I'm going to have to actually light my prop. Just as the end catches and the cherry glows, my "contact" comes around the corner.

"You smoke now, Daisy? I feel like I don't even know you." Erick chuckles as he strides toward me.

I wasn't expecting him to be in civilian clothes. I can assure you, I'm not disappointed.

He stops in the darkness just beyond the pool of light cast by the single caged bulb above the metal door. "It's probably best if I keep out of sight."

"Whatever you say, officer." I fully embody the flirtatious character of Daisy and sway my hips as I approach my partially obscured rendezvous.

He shoves his hands in the pockets of his just-right jeans. "I thought I'd stop by and save you the trouble of eavesdropping all night. The gang made their second hit tonight."

"Gosh darn it, if that ain't as frustrating as hen poop on a pump handle."

He chuckles. "How do you come up with this stuff?"

"Daisy is a very colorful character," I whisper as I lean toward him.

The back door busts open and Lars shouts, "Daisy, breaks over. I'm drowning—" When he catches sight of me locking lips with some rando in the alley, he stops short and heads back inside.

As soon as the door closes, I pull myself away

from Erick and stare with all kinds of tingly shock. "What the actual—"

His face is so red, I can feel the heat, and he brushes his lips nervously. "I didn't know what to do. I couldn't risk him seeing me. He'd recognize me in a heartbeat."

"So your solution was to just plant a kiss on Daisy, like you've known her all your life?"

He slips his arm around my waist. "I wasn't kissing Daisy."

My whole body flashes with heat and I'm sure there are beads of sweat forming along the edges of my wig. "Um, all right, whatever. I have to get back inside."

I spin out of his grasp and race into the bar. My heart is pounding, and I can't think clearly.

That was our first kiss. Was it? That's not how I wanted it to be. I wanted it to be grand, and romantic, and perfect. Not some informant slobbering on her handler in a seedy alley.

"Daisy!"

No time to think. Just time to drink.

The raucous table in the corner has decided to challenge me to a shots contest. Prior to moving to Pin Cherry, I would've been able to put that whole table down without breaking a sweat. Now that I'm nearly a teetotaler, I'm not sure how long I can hang on. But there's a lot of money in shots, so I take their bet.

As I'm loading up the tray, Lars sets a square shot glass on the tray. "That gets filled with water. Just make sure you always drink out of this glass and then watch 'em fall like dominoes."

I look over and grin at the proprietor. "Honey, y'all are as sneaky as a water moccasin in tall grass 'round here." I walk over to the corner, pass out the shots, and shout, "Drink!"

"Down the hatch," they reply.

I tap my empty glass twice on the table, and they all hurry to copy my action.

"Another round!" yells the handsy bald guy on my left.

"You got it."

After five rounds, three of their group are looking very green around the gills, and the other four aren't far behind.

It's only fair I help push them over the edge after they were so inappropriate with my behind. "What d'y'all say to one more round, boys?"

There are several groans and a couple of headshakes.

I'm willing to do just about anything to seal this deal. "Last round's on the house, what d'ya say?"

Most of the table rallies and gives a drunken cheer.

I tray up another round of shots.

Lars sidles up next to me behind the bar. "That's coming out of your tips."

"It's absolutely worth it, darlin'." I return to the table, distribute the shots, and shout, "Drink!" As I tap my empty on the table twice, the rest of the dominoes fall.

Scooping up the discarded shot glasses, I walk away with a little extra swish-swish in my wiggle.

"Last call!" Lars props open the front door and starts physically escorting our inebriated patrons outside. He calls to me, "If they don't buy a drink, they don't get to stay and play."

"You got it."

"You don't have to go home, but you can't stay here." He repeats the mantra with each group he chaperones out of our establishment.

When we count out the tips, I'm left with nearly $500, even after we subtract the round of shots.

I fold up the money and shove it in my pocket with pride. I'd almost forgotten how good it feels to do an honest day's work. Of course, that's not what Daisy would say. She says, "Well, that is a right fine stack of cabbage. It's a pleasure doing business with you, Lars."

He nods. "I bet you could sell ice to Eskimos with that smile."

I avert my gaze in a classic humble but shocked expression. "I'll see ya tomorrow night, Mr. Bossman."

"Good night, Daisy."

The last bus ran two hours ago. Despite the cool breeze, it's still a beautiful night. The moon is about a quarter full and it's just bright enough to see one foot in front of the other between the sparse streetlights.

I had hoped that a brisk walk would help clear my head. But all it's doing is giving me endless opportunities to replay the scene from the alley.

Erick in those absolutely perfect jeans.

Erick smelling all citrus and woodsy, and a little bit sweaty.

Erick's loose bangs falling over his face as he leans toward me.

Erick's lips on mine.

Maybe it wasn't as bad as I thought. Maybe it was just right. I could try to replay the scene accessing my extrasensory perceptions, but I'm worried the intensity of the real emotions we were both feeling might knock me straight onto my backside. I better wait till I'm home safe in bed to replay that version of the movie.

CHAPTER 14

WHEN MY DAD'S call wakes me at the ungodly hour of 9:00 a.m., I'm not the least bit upset. Not only did I have the best night's sleep of my life, but also the dreams were—let's say, "memorable." I kick my covers off and swoop my phone to my ear like a movie star vamping for her paparazzi.

"Good morning, dearest father Duncan."

My blissed-out greeting is met with a mild choking sound that I think I've heard referred to as a "chortle."

"What?" I mentally review my greeting. "Oh, I hear it now. Let's forget I said that, and chalk it up to still having one foot in dreamland. So, what's up, Dad?"

"I want you to come down and have a look at the crime scene. It's not that I don't trust the FBI and local law enforcement, but you have a special set of skills—"

Sporting my very best "terrible Irish accent," I launch into my impression of Liam Neeson. "But what I do have are a very particular set of skills."

Jacob and I share a laugh.

"If I steal some of Pyewacket's Fruity Puffs—" I glance around the room surreptitiously, but see no sign of my furry friend "—I can be there in half an hour."

"Meet me at the depot and I'll drive you out to the siding where the cars have been sequestered."

"Copy that."

I happily slip into my regular Mitzy Moon attire, rake a hand through my hair, and put on a little moisturizing lip tint. By the time I reach the back room to steal some sugared cereal, I hear Grams giving Pyewacket her version of a lecture.

"And you scared me half to death, Mr. Cuddlekins. That's quite a feat considering I'm already dead. Your constant snooping is worse than Mitzy. Between the two of you, I can't get a moment's rest."

I step into the back room. "Now you know how I feel. I'm sure you and Pye can come to some understanding. I'm off to see if I can pick up any psychic messages from last night's train robbery remains."

She gasps and covers her mouth. "Sweetie, it all sounds so dangerous. I'm not sure if this is the best way to use your powers. Maybe you should focus on finding lost pets, saving children, or holding séances for the bereaved."

"Wow, you're really stuck in some nostalgia loop. Doc Ledo said that Pyewacket has at least six good lives left, and, for your information, I have promised to save one child. Besides, Dad asked for the favor and he'll be with me the whole time. How could I possibly be unsafe when I'm being protected by your strapping son?"

Grams crosses her arms over her ample bosom and tilts her head back and forth as she weighs my evidence. "I suppose there's a ring of truth to that. Tonight's the last night I want you working at that terrible tavern, though. Clearly those nasty robbers aren't coming back in, and exposing yourself to that kind of place and those kinds of behaviors is just plain foolish."

"I'm on a case, Grams. It's not my style to quit while there are still clues to be gathered."

She vanishes into thin air, but her voice echoes from the void. "No one cares about the ghost's feelings."

I scratch Pyewacket between the ears, pour him a large portion of Fruity Puffs, and sneak a few handfuls into a baggie for the drive.

I park behind the train depot, making sure that I won't be visible, in case Lars happens to be working over at Final Destination.

As I approach the back door, I suddenly recall that I have a key to this place. The story is that my grandpa Cal gave it to Grams when they were married and she "forgot" to return it after they were divorced. I had to use the key once before, when I was searching for clues to my grandfather's killer and desperately trying to clear my own name, so I know it works. I let myself in and run upstairs to the office that now belongs to my dad.

The room never fails to impress. Encased in thick, gleaming glass, the office looks over the entire train station. The converted building houses office space, conference rooms, a break room, and part of the original terminal has been preserved as a display housing a shining vintage steam engine.

As I make my way toward the Viking statue in the corner, I ask. "How do you like the digs?"

Jacob looks up. "Hey, Hannah didn't let me know you'd arrived."

"Yeah, about that. I came in through the back."

"But that's . . . Never mind, don't tell me. If my baby girl knows how to pick locks that's none of my business."

I dangle my keychain and grin. "Actually, I have the key. Courtesy of your mom."

He shakes his head. "Of course you do. Well, let's load up in my truck and head down to the box-cars. I sure hope you get some messages. They got away with over half a million in high-end elec-tronics last night. It definitely makes Midwest Union look bad, and it's certainly not a big endorse-ment for our policy to hire ex-cons."

"I had no idea items that valuable were shipped by rail."

My dad laughs and leads the way out to the parking lot. "That's nothing. A shipment of phones is worth two million. Besides, how do you think things get from the coasts of our country to all the landlocked consumers?"

"Drones?"

"Millennials." He rolls his eyes for my benefit. "Get in the truck. This may be one of the few times I'm actually going to know more about something than you. Pay attention; railroading is in your blood."

We drive about forty minutes southwest of Pin Cherry and the countryside has definitely gained in elevation.

As if reading my mind, my father gives me a few more details about the robbery. "I've got to hand it to these guys, they are absolute profession-als. They scoped out at least a hundred miles of rail and found the exact place where the combination of an uphill grade and a very sharp turn means a slow-moving target that's invisible to the conductor. They were able to hit five cars before the track straightened out, and I assume they loaded their haul into some trucks and drove away.

"Like semi trucks?"

"According to the FBI they started out using pickup trucks on the East Coast, but as they got more successful, they clearly upgraded their vehicles. The size of their hauls keeps getting larger. The pattern of three hits indicates a level of confidence that you just don't find with underfunded amateurs."

I nod.

"The interval between the three hits is completely unpredictable. There's no pattern. So we could be in for another hit tonight or it could be two weeks from now."

"That really sucks, Dad. I'm sorry this is happening and I'm really sorry about the timing. Just when you're giving your program a start. Do you think any of your second-chance guys are involved?"

"I wish I could say unequivocally 'no way,' but recidivism is a real thing. So, all I can say is that I hope not."

I really don't want to tell him what I overheard at Final D. I mean, just because two criminals men-

tioned a contact that had done time doesn't neces-
sarily mean it's one of my dad's Restorative Justice
guys.

Jacob looks over at me. "Why do you ask? Did
you have a vision or something?"

"So, I hate to mention it, but I did overhear a
couple of guys down at the roadhouse talking about
paying off someone at the depot for information.
They said the guy did time in Clearwater."

Jacob sighs and his shoulders pinch with tension. "Of course, I hope it's not one of my guys,
Mitzy, but I have to put the needs of the railroad
ahead of my own. When I took on this idea to give
guys like me a second chance, I had to accept the
very real possibility that there would be more fail-
ures than successes. If one of my guys is on the take,
I need to let Sheriff Harper know. Any link to the
train robbers could be the difference between
solving this case, or watching this gang get away
—again."

"I'm sorry. I really wanted to pretend I never
heard it. But I guess that wouldn't help any of us."

We turn off the asphalt onto a dirt road, and I
can see the five railcars surrounded by yellow tape
and guarded by two of our local deputies whom I
vaguely recognize, but I've never had the pleasure
of meeting.

We park and walk toward the boxcars.

The taller of the two deputies steps forward and dramatically puts up his hand, as though he's one of the Supremes. "Sorry, this is an active crime scene. No one is allowed past the yellow tape."

"Well, this guy is Jacob Duncan, the owner of the railroad, and I'm his daughter and a personal friend of Sheriff Harper. I'm sure you'll find we're allowed to walk anywhere we'd like."

The deputy doesn't budge.

I hear my father exhale behind me. "My daughter and I need to do a quick inventory for the insurance claim. We won't be removing anything from the site and we'll be out of your hair in no time."

Surprisingly my father's approach receives a lowering of the "stop" hand, a lifting of the yellow tape, and a wave through.

We climb into the first car, and my ring turns to an icy circle on my finger. I glance down and see the image of a boxcar door sliding open. Not particularly helpful. But a question does pop into my head from nowhere. "How do they get in? Aren't the doors secured somehow?"

My father nods. "The doors are secured, but the locks could be cut with almost any consumer-grade bolt cutter. Modern-day train robberies aren't that common, and security is mainly a deterrent, designed to ward off amateurs.

"Can you show me one of these locks?" I'm not sure why I'm obsessing about the locks. Sometimes my psychic sense of knowing comes with very little explanation.

My dad hops out and walks down the row of cars. "There's a piece in this one, Mitzy."

The deputy steps over and looks down the train.

I wave. "We're almost done." Jogging over to my father, he points to a chunk of the lock that was wedged in to keep the boxcar door open. As soon as I see it, a series of images hits me like a freight train. Ironic, right?

He must recognize the catatonic expression that seizes my features, because he waits patiently until I gasp for air and resurface.

"What did you see?"

"I saw them cutting locks, I saw them sliding out all the boxes and crates, I saw them loading everything into two semi trucks that left in opposite directions. But this is the key." I point to the thick piece of red plastic wedged into the door track.

"What do you mean? These locks come in a bunch of colors, all mixed in a large bin. Why is this the key?"

"It has to be the key, because Pyewacket had to be rushed into surgery to remove a piece of red plastic, just like this, from his throat. You and I both know that's not a coincidence. Not in this family."

My father nods slowly. "You're right. Not in this family."

"Who locks the loaded cars?"

"Could be any one of ten or fifteen different guys. Why?"

"What if the color means something to the gang? What if the high-value cars are the only ones locked with these red locks. It would make it so much easier for them to hit the right cars in such a short window."

My dad smiles proudly. "See, you're way ahead of the FBI."

"Now what?"

"Now I pass along this information to the FBI and maybe they'll have some ideas."

I put a hand on my father's arm to pull him to a stop. "Or . . ."

CHAPTER 15

ON THE DRIVE back to civilization, I continue to lay out my plan, and I take it as a true compliment when my dad says I could've been a criminal mastermind. Even though I'm certain he meant it as a cautionary tale.

"Maybe I should question the second-chance guys and see if I pick up any psychic messages."

Jacob nods. "The only guy working today is Anthony, I think. I'll check the schedule for the other one's shifts. The two guys working at the Restorative Justice office wouldn't have any info about the railcars, but I did get two men placed in positions down at the docks." He taps his fingers on the steering wheel. "We'll figure it out."

From the three-hundred-and-sixty-degree vantage point of my father's office at the depot, he points out the tattooed head of Anthony Jenkins. "You walk down and chat with him. I'll wait outside."

I raise my eyebrows.

"I hate to say it, but the guilty tend to run."

"Oh, right."

I casually wander down to the main floor and walk toward my target. He looks so much bigger at eye level. "Hey, Anthony, I'm Jacob's daughter, Mitzy Moon."

He gives my outstretched hand a friendly shake. "What can I do for you, Miss Moon?"

Definitely wanting to err on the side of caution with this guy, I take the friendliest approach I can imagine. "I know how this is going to sound, so I'm gonna apologize for that in advance. But I have to ask."

He nods slowly. There's a nervous shift in his energy, which flashes a warning to the hairs on the back of my neck.

"Somebody in the yard is taking money for an illegal side gig, so my dad figures he needs to tighten down security. Have you seen anything suspicious lately?"

Anthony wrings his hands, and I feel his adrenaline spike. Even without the help of my extrasensory perception, I'm pretty sure this guy's about to run. As soon as the opportunity presents itself, Anthony pushes past me and makes a break for it, but my father is waiting near the exit and grabs him as soon as he bolts out the door.

The large man looks small with my dad's massive hands gripping his arm.

"Look, Anthony, I'm here to help you. Remember that. Just tell me what you know. If there's any way I can keep your name out of it, I will. All right?"

Anthony struggles for a moment before exhaling in defeat. "Look, man, it was just the one time and I needed the money. I didn't do anything illegal, you know?"

My dad and I exchange a glance before he asks, "What did you do?

"I took this group of rich guys fishing. My pop used to take me all the time when I was a kid, and I know the best spots. They all caught more than their limit, and I just looked the other way." He shifts his weight back and forth and rubs a hand over his face. "I got two little kids, Jacob. You know my situation."

My father's shoulders relax and a caring smile softens his face. "Anthony, I understand the situation. But if you want the Foundation to make a positive report to your parole officer, you gotta keep your nose clean, man. We don't want the first group of second-chance guys going straight back to jail. Understood?"

Anthony nods vigorously. "I can give them back the money. It won't happen again."

Before my father can answer, I jump in. "Why don't you donate it to the animal shelter. They can always use a little help with the new puppies this time of year." I glance over at Jacob and ask, "Will that settle his account with you, Dad?"

He nods, and a proud smile turns up the corner of his mouth.

By the time we finish our interrogation/counseling session, I barely have time to race back to the bookshop, swap out my T-shirt for a slutty tank top, and hastily pin my red wig into place.

There's definitely no time for me to catch the bus, so I'm forced to beg and plead until Twiggy reluctantly agrees to drop me off a couple of blocks from the bar.

Lars avoids making eye contact when I show up, and in place of our usual small talk an awkward silence hangs between us.

I run through my "Daisy" accent in my mind and launch into an apology. "I want ya to know, I'm real sorry about that guy in the alley last night. It was nothing, and I won't let it happen again."

"Hey, Daisy, I'm not trying to be your dad or whatever. But most of the guys that come in this bar don't deserve the time of day. I'd just hate to see you get hurt, that's all."

"Well, I sure do appreciate you being so sweet about it. Like I said, won't happen again."

The mood lightens and Lars heads into the supply room to fill ice buckets while I wipe down the tables and sweep the floor.

The crowd's a little lighter tonight and the pace is far more manageable. I'm definitely getting into a nice relaxed rhythm when I notice Scarface and Ponytail slide onto a couple of stools at the end of the bar.

I can't believe the nerve. They just robbed my dad, and they walk in here to have a drink like they don't have a care in the world. I have half a mind to spit in their whiskey. But then I remember there's only one heist left and this might be my last chance to get some useful information.

I crack a beer and set it down in front of one of the regulars. "Got any good stories for me, darlin'?"

He takes a long pull on the beer, sets it down, and shakes his head. "Nothing good never happens 'round here." He picks at the dirt under his thick, ridged fingernails.

"That's not what I heard."

He leans forward eagerly. "What did you hear?"

I lean across the bar, but instead of lowering my

voice I raise it a little to make sure the boys at the end of the bar can hear my juicy gossip.

"When I was in that holding cell at the sheriff's station, I heard something about a train robbery!"

My clueless shill whistles and lifts his bushy brown eyebrows in surprise. "Around here?"

"Near as I could tell. They said it was a real amateur operation." My words have the desired effect, and the cocky blowhards at the end of the bar look my way.

I wink and move toward them. "What can I get you fellas?"

The one with the dark hair and the face scar is sulky and defensive. "Did I hear you talking about a train robbery?"

"You sure did. Why? Did y'all hear something?"

His ponytail-wearing friend elbows him in the ribs, but that doesn't stop him from defending his honor. "I heard it was a real professional job. Pretty big haul, and no evidence." His chin juts out defensively.

"Shoot, I don't know where y'all heard that, darlin'. Talk down at the sheriff's station made it seem like a couple of real small-time operators. Sounded like the deputies would have 'em rounded up in a couple days. That don't seem very big-time to me."

Ponytail reaches across the bar and grabs my wrist. "What exactly did you hear, girlie?"

The waves of threatening energy rolling off him make the hairs on the back of my neck spike as a warning chill drips down my spine. I try to pull my wrist away but he squeezes tighter. "Hey, you're hurting me."

Lars looks up from delivering beers to the pool tables and makes a beeline for the two troublemakers. He puts a firm hand on Ponytail's shoulder. "It's probably best if you take your hand off my waitress."

The felon's eyes narrow, and he glares at me with frightening malice, but he loosens his grip and I yank my hand away.

"Any more trouble outta you two, and I'll have to ask you to leave." Lars's thick sausage fingers clamp down firmly to emphasize his point.

Ponytail mumbles something under his breath, and I notice the bulge of a gun in a shoulder holster under his jacket as he jerks out from under the owner's hand.

Time for Daisy to diffuse the situation. "It's no bother, Lars. We were all just chattin'. Y'all settle down and I'll bring a couple shots of whiskey on the house."

Lars exhales and stomps away.

Ponytail wipes his mouth with the back of his hand and says, "That's more like it."

I pour the shots, and by the time I return to deliver them, a new patron in a hoodie has taken a stool a couple of slots over from "crook's corner."

"What can I get you, honey?"

The man looks up and pushes his hood back as he ponders his answer.

Uh oh. I'd recognize that skull ink anywhere. It's Anthony.

His eyes scan my face, and before I have time for a secret signal, a hair toss or a silly southern colloquialism, I clock his look of recognition.

"Hey, you're Jacob Duncan's daughter?"

"I think you must have me confused with someone else, darlin'. I'm not from 'round here."

He doesn't take the brushoff or get the clue. "No, no we met at the train station. Don't you remember me chatting with you and your dad today?"

All the hope in the world isn't going to erase that phrase. I see Ponytail reach inside his jacket.

I turn to make a run for the back door, but he pulls his gun and waves it threateningly at the patrons. "I'm taking that redhead, and I'm walking out of here. You want to die today? Get in my way."

His buddy with the scar on his left cheek walks around behind the bar, grabs my arm firmly, and yanks me toward the front door.

Ponytail continues to threaten patrons with his loaded gun.

As the door creaks open, I make one last desperate attempt. "Lars, call Sheriff—"

A large, sweaty hand clamps down over my mouth and the next thing I know, I'm lying in the trunk of a car, looking up as Ponytail slams the lid shut.

CHAPTER 16

WHEN I SIGNED the CI paperwork absolving Birch County for any and all things that could go wrong during my work as a confidential informant, I'd be lying if I said that this scenario crossed my mind. I mean, when you read the line about "up to and including death," who actually thinks that's a legit possibility?

If you're looking for a silver lining, it's that I have plenty of "alone time" to review the choices that brought me to this point. I've come to the conclusion that Daisy isn't any better at keeping herself out of trouble than Mitzy.

I hope Lars has enough sense to call the sheriff. That is, if he's not too angry about being deceived. I'm sure Anthony, the blabbermouth at the bar, told him who I really am.

Before we dive too deeply into the darkness of my abduction, let's not forget the highlight of good news: I flushed out the train robbers.

Yay me. I pump my fists in a pathetic celebratory gesture inside my mobile coffin.

The bad news is, I won't be pulling any super-spy phone tracking maneuvers since Scarface ripped the phone out of my back pocket and smashed it in the parking lot back at Final Destination.

There must be something that could help me in the tens of thousands of hours of television locked away in my foster-child brain.

Think. Think. Think.

This is so *Jimmy Neutron.*

Not helpful.

Think something useful.

There was a program about teaching children . . . It's all coming back to me.

I remember some daytime TV program about teaching children to fight back against kidnappers. Yes! Rule number one: The best time to get away is before they grab you.

Looks like I failed that part of the training.

They also recommended a lot of kicking, biting, and screaming for help.

Also not particularly useful to me now.

Wait, I remember something about kicking out a taillight. I might be able to do that.

I orient myself in the dark trunk and kick at what I think could be the taillight.

Hooray. I've succeeded in possibly breaking my toe. But that's about it.

There were specific methods of escape that were different between older cars and newer cars, but I didn't even get a good look at what kind of car they threw me into.

Shame, that.

I feel around and there's no safety release for the trunk lock, so I guess that rules out a newer car. But, as I explore around the dark, smelly trunk with my hands, I do encounter some wires.

That's something.

I start yanking and pulling all the wires I can.

A sudden bump jostles me severely, and I bang my head on the trunk lid as we bounce through a deep rut, off the asphalt road, and onto a dirt lane. The smell of dust fills the small space as gravel pings off the rear quarter panels.

Great.

It hardly seems important whether or not they have taillights when they're sure to be the only car on the road.

I wish I knew where they were taking me. I

wish I could pop out one of these taillights and leave a trail of breadcrumbs.

Frustration and fear grip me, and I place a few more desperate kicks into the corner, but to no avail.

Time to abandon my escape strategy and start thinking about survival.

All of my struggling feels like it's sucked the air out of the trunk, and I'm sweaty and claustrophobic. And this infernal wig itches like mad.

I reach up to rip it off my head, when the magic mood ring on my left hand burns hot. I pull it toward my face in time to see a bobby pin.

Boy, this ring has really been going for the obvious lately.

Yes, my wig is held on with several bobby pins. That's hardly a newsflash. As I reach up a second time to pull off the wig, the hairs on the back of my neck stand on end and the possible uses of a bobby pin race through my mind in a series of lock picking sequences from some of my favorite detective shows.

On second thought, I'll leave the wig on and keep my secret stash of bobby pins hidden, for now.

The fact is, Scarface and Ponytail have no idea whether Jacob Duncan's daughter has red hair or not. They just heard the guy at the bar out me. It's not like they recognized me. I may as well keep the disguise and the accent for as long as possible.

For some reason, known only to my psychic senses, I reach up and pull one bobby pin from the wig and slip it into my bra. Seems like a good idea to have a backup plan at this point.

The ruts in the road are definitely getting deeper, and my uncomfortable ride in the trunk is becoming positively painful. I don't know how much longer my body can take this jolting abuse.

Fortunately, the misery ends in a few more minutes. I mean, this misery ends. I shudder to think what awaits in the train robbers' hideout.

The trunk lid pops open, and my captors are dimly outlined by the faint moonlight. Ponytail holds the gun while Scarface yanks me out of the trunk.

In keeping with my plan to preserve my cover, I stick with a southern accent. "Y'all don't have to be so rough. I ain't fightin' you."

Neither of them says a word as they drag me to the cabin.

The door opens and four more ruffians, seated around a 1970s-style Formica kitchen table, look up angrily.

But what catches my eye is the man with his arm around a frightened young boy, sitting quietly on the plaid sofa.

My stomach twists into knots. Looking similar to their pictures on Karen's phone, it has to be her son and the abusive ex-husband.

It was bad enough when I thought I just had myself to protect, but I promised not to let anything happen to that little boy.

New plan: Do whatever they say and get that little guy out of here alive.

An older bald guy with an impressively detailed neck tattoo stands up and glares at Ponytail and Scarface. I'm going to go out on a limb and assume this guy is in charge.

"Tell me again why you two idiots thought it was a good idea to bring this chick back here."

Scarface and his ego pipe up defensively. "Turns out she's the daughter of the guy who owns the railroad. And she heard some stuff at the police station. I thought we could get some information and maybe a ransom."

The big bald guy strides across the bare wooden floor of the small kitchen and punches Scarface right in his, well, scarred face.

The guy goes down hard, and Ponytail aims his gun at the boss.

His voice wavers, but he holds the gun steady. "Don't pull any of that crap with me. He was popping off and I figured she knew too much. She could identify us."

The man I'm going to name "The Tank" turns on Ponytail and growls. "Identify us as what? Did you tell her you robbed the train?"

"No. Never." Ponytail glances at the man on the floor. "He was just saying stuff about how the train robbery was all professional and whatever."

The Tank steps menacingly toward the gun. The steel barrel presses a dent in his chest between his intimidating pecs. He has no fear of death. "Exactly. She didn't know anything. You idiots brought back a problem, not a solution."

Hopefully, I might be able to head off their ransom plan at the pass. "I hate to interrupt y'all, but my dad and I aren't real close. I don't think he's gonna pay—"

The Tank grabs me by the throat. "You don't talk. Got it."

I nod my head as best I can with his giant meat hook around my neck.

He releases me and shoves me toward the couch. "Sit down over there, with the rest of the disposable baggage."

CHAPTER 17

N<small>O</small> C<small>OMFORTABLE</small> A<small>CCOMMODATIONS</small> A<small>RE</small> O<small>FFERED</small>. I huddle at one end of the scratchy plaid couch, while the father and son occupy the other.

The Tank generously sets up a schedule for watching us until dawn.

Gosh, what a host.

There may have been a point during the dead of night when I dozed off for a solid twenty minutes, otherwise every one of my regular and extra senses is on high alert.

There's no conversation as our captors change shifts, but I do sense uneasiness, irritation, and even fear when Scarface reports for his turn at guard duty.

The Tank scheduled himself for the morning

shift, so when the sun makes its appearance, "Daisy" offers to be of use.

"If you beg my pardon, sir, I could make y'all some breakfast."

My offer surprises him, but I can hear his stomach growling with just my regular old human ears.

He nods. "Don't try anything."

"Not a thing." I look through the refrigerator and see that it's luckily well-stocked with eggs and bacon. I begin a search of the cupboards for a large bowl.

A quietly frustrated voice whispers from the couch. "Mixing bowls are in the cupboard next to the sink. Under the counter."

Either he was previously assigned cook duties or he's been to this cabin before. Information to store for later.

I retrieve a bowl and whip up my egg mixture, while heating a large frying pan.

My search doesn't reveal any signs of coffee, but there is a coffee maker.

"Y'all have coffee?"

The Tank crosses his arms over his massive chest. "Freezer."

Opening the freezer, I see a family-size can of Chock full o' Nuts. That'll have to do. I make a few quick calculations based on the size of the coffee maker and the number of people I've seen in the cabin, and get the first pot of java brewing.

I cook the bacon first and transfer it to a plate to drain, while I quickly scramble up the eggs. Foster family number six was big on buying groceries but not real big on using them. I learned to cook a variety of basic meals, mostly just to keep myself alive, during that stint.

As the aroma of brewing coffee, frying bacon, and scrambled eggs wafts through the small cabin, five sleepy gangsters make their way to the table to join their boss. I serve them coffee, and set a bowl of sugar and, what I hope isn't expired, creamer on the table.

As they yawn and stretch themselves awake, I serve up breakfast. However, I take the first plate of food to The Tank. He looks up at me and his eyes narrow, but I see a hint of a smirk.

My psychic senses pick up on a flash of admiration. Lucky for me I guessed right.

I serve the rest of the posse before I make a plate for the father and son. I walk slowly toward the sagging couch. Every fiber of my being is waiting for a shout, and I'm hoping I'm not about to lose any favor I've gained.

Fortunately, the crew is tucked into their breakfasts and they don't seem to care that I'm feeding the prisoners.

I manage to scarf down a strip of bacon and a couple of mouthfuls of eggs before The Tank calls for seconds.

Grabbing the frying pan and the spatula, I walk toward him. If he were the only one, it would be so easy to crack this cast-iron skillet across the side of his head. Whoa! Where did that come from? I need to get my Angelina Jolie under control and keep playing this room like the genteel Southern belle I'm supposed to be.

A couple of the thugs actually bring their dishes to the sink and I can barely suppress my urge to make a wisecrack. Instead, I run a sink of hot water and busy myself with post-breakfast cleanup.

"Anybody got a cigarette?" Not sure if they'll fall for it, but I'd really love to get outside and see if I can figure out where we're at.

Ponytail slides his chair back from the table. "I'm having a smoke." He pats the gun in his holster. "Follow me."

We walk outside and he tamps his pack of old-school non-filters twice in the palm of his hand before he dumps out two sticks. He puts one in his mouth and hands the other one to me.

As he pulls the lighter out of his pocket, my chest tightens. I hope I can pull off a puff or two without coughing like a complete newbie.

Surprisingly, he offers to light my cigarette first.

"You seem like a smart girl. You keep making yourself useful, the boss might take you with us."

Super. My options are try to escape and die, stick around and be uncooperative and die, or make myself useful and get conscripted into a gang of train robbers.

Hooray.

I hold the cigarette like every cool girl in every movie I've ever seen. "Thanks for the tip, darlin'." The small log cabin is made from whole trees, notched together at the corners. The foundation is a hodge-podge of split rocks, probably from this property. If I weren't being held hostage in it, I'd say it's a quaint and cozy little cottage.

Ponytail walks over to kick a tire on a black SUV.

I glance around and look for neighbors. None. The cabin is totally isolated. It's located very close to the lakeshore, but there's not another cabin in sight, not even across the lake. I take a couple of steps toward the corner of the building to get a better look, and Ponytail grabs my arm and squeezes hard.

His grip makes my skin crawl, besides the fact that it really hurts.

"I ain't goin' nowhere. Just wanted to see the lake. I haven't been in these parts long and there's just so many lakes everywhere. Kinda beautiful."

He doesn't remove his hand from my arm, but he loosens his grip and pushes me in front of him to the corner of the cabin. I gaze out at the lake. It looks like there's land in the middle of the lake, or maybe it's a very strangely shaped lake. "Is that an island?"

He takes a long drag on his cigarette and exhales a series of smoke rings before he answers. "There's actually two out there."

I'm not sure how many lakes with two islands there are within roughly a forty-minute radius of Pin Cherry, but I will definitely lock that little tidbit away.

He finishes his cigarette and drops it on the ground—still glowing.

Having grown up in the desert, and lived through a number of major forest fires, I'm completely unable to leave a lit cigarette outdoors. I grind my heel on the butt.

He laughs. "Women."

I grind out my own cigarette, and he pushes me ahead of him back into the cabin.

The Tank looks toward us as the screen door slams. "Any trouble?"

Ponytail pats his holster and grins. "Not a one, boss."

The men are gathered around the table, and The Tank seems to be going over the plan for the

next heist. It surprises me that they're brazenly discussing their strategy in front of us. However, that's
a stomach-turning confirmation that they don't plan
to leave us alive. I guess they're feeling pretty cocky.

As I listen, I don't hear anything useful. They're
simply talking about who does what, and what
items are high value. Televisions and phones.

One of the three men who I have yet to nickname gestures toward the three of us gathered on
the couch, leans toward The Tank, and whispers
something. The Tank nods and turns toward us.
"The three of you head into the back bedroom."

We stand obediently, and I follow the man
whom I'm assuming is a returning visitor to the
cabin into the back bedroom.

The Tank pulls the door shut behind and a key
clicks in the lock.

The three of us sit quietly while voices rise and
fall in the kitchen.

Eventually things go silent, and I wonder if
they've left us alone. Time to take my first risk.

I keep my voice very soft and low, but choose to
protect my cover, not knowing much about my sup-
posedly fellow captives. "Hey y'all, my name's
Daisy. I had the misfortune of servin' a couple of
these boys drinks at Final Destination. Apparently,
they didn't care for my bartending skills and next

thing I know, I'm in their trunk." I finish with a friendly smile and an encouraging nod.

The father puts a protective arm around the son and pulls him close. "Name's Denny. Cabin belonged to my uncle. My cousins and me used to hang out here every summer. Brought my son back to show him my old stomping grounds and teach him how to fish." He shakes his head. "When we got here, I saw the boards had been taken off the windows and I walked in and found two of those thugs sitting in my living room like they owned the place." He grimaces with disgust.

I shake my head and murmur my dismay. Something feels off in his story, but my psychic senses don't offer any clarity. Maybe he's playing his cards close to the vest—like me.

Denny continues. "The one with the ponytail pulled his gun, then the next thing you know, me and Breck are hostages. They have me cooking and cleaning while they rob trains. They even sent me into town to get supplies for them one time, but they kept Breck here—at gunpoint." He bows his head and I sense that he feels guilty.

"You did the right thing. Y'hear? You protected your son. Any man in your position woulda done the same."

"I guess. Still can't believe they took the cabin."

"Don't lose hope, darlin'. We'll figure something out."

He looks at me wistfully for a moment, before his eyes return to the worried stare of earlier.

"So you're from 'round here, Denny?"

"Farther south, but I spent a lot of time up here before I joined the Army. Haven't been back in a while."

All the pieces are fitting together. The story, the face, the beard, the crooked nose. This is absolutely Karen's ex-husband and the missing child. No sense letting him in on what I know. Seems like a much better idea to get as much information as I can from him. "So how far are we from Pin Cherry?"

"It's a good forty-five minutes, in the summer. In the winter, you gotta park out on the main road and snowshoe in, or bring the trailer with the sled."

Now Mitzy happens to know that a "sled" is another word for a snowmobile. But I'd have to assume "Daisy" does not. "Darlin', forgive me, what's a sled?"

A slight smile breaks the tension on his face. "That's a term they use for snowmobiles up north."

I crouch to the child's eye level and smile warmly at Breck. "Have you ever ridden on a sled?"

Breck shakes his head.

My extra senses pick up on the fear and trepidation that all this trauma has lodged in this poor little boy's heart. I pace around the small room and continue with my friendly interview. "Is there any chance of a boat out back?"

"Sure. But she hasn't been in the water in at least a decade. Might be pretty leaky. And I'm sure there's no gas in the engine. My cousins stopped coming up here after my uncle passed."

"All right. We'll keep thinking." I take a few more laps around the small room. "Is your car here?"

"Yeah, that Chevy suburban out front is mine. They took the keys as soon as we walked in."

"Y'all didn't happen to see where they put 'em, did ya?"

"No. That big bald one probably keeps them in his pocket. He doesn't trust anybody. Not even his own crew."

Now, that's a helpful piece of information. "And who would y'all say is most chatty?"

Denny looks up at me and smiles. "Has to be the guy with the scar on his cheek."

"That does make sense. That Scarface couldn't keep his mouth shut at the bar. That could come in handy."

For the first time since I've arrived, I see Denny straighten his spine and take a deep breath. "I was just a grunt in the Army, but I'm pretty good with hand-to-hand combat."

I walk forward and place a hand on his shoulder. "I'd like to figure us a way outta here without it havin' to come to that."

I dart my eyes meaningfully toward Breck and shrug.

He seems to receive my meaning as he pulls his son closer. "Yeah, it'd be nice to just slip away."

I nod fervently. "Now you're cooking with gas."

I haven't heard so much as a cough from the kitchen in over half an hour. There's a chance that they left us alone.

Stepping toward the door, I press my ear to the wood. There's nothing but silence out there.

Carefully slipping the bobby pin from my bra, I begin my attempt to pick the lock. My foster brother trained me with a hook pick and a tension wrench, but I made do with a hairpin or paperclip once or twice. I'm just hoping to get lucky.

A small scared voice whispers from the bed, "Can you pick locks?"

I stop, glance over my shoulder, and smile broadly. "Most of the time. That's our little secret, all right."

Breck nods his head and I see a tiny spark of promise flicker in his eye.

Charlie's Angels! I hope I can pick this lock and save that little boy.

After a few unsuccessful attempts, I finally feel

the pins slide above the sheer line, and, with a little pressure, the lock turns.

Slipping the bobby pin back into my bra, I twist the handle as slowly and quietly as possible. Turning, I put one finger over my lips in a silent shushing gesture to my co-prisoners.

Inching the door open, I pop my head around and continue listening and looking. As I step out, I carefully pull the door closed behind me.

When I walk into the kitchen, I see Scarface asleep on the couch. I methodically walk heel-to-toe, heel-to-toe, evenly distributing my weight as I move toward the front door.

Unfortunately, a loose board creaks loudly one stride from my goal.

He bolts upright. "Where the heck do you think you're going?"

I spin around and fake surprise. "Aunt Jemima! I was just getting some water. Can I fetch you anything?"

He eyes me suspiciously. "How did you get out of the bedroom?"

I smile as innocently as possible. "I just opened the door, darlin'. Honestly, I was thirsty. Can I get you some water, or sweet tea?"

For some reason, he believes me. "Yeah, I'll take some water. No ice."

I fill two glasses with tap water and a sudden

thought strikes me. The truth symbols! Silas taught me a special set of alchemical symbols that, when combined, can transmute an ordinary glass of liquid into truth serum. I haven't been practicing as much as I should, but there's no time like the present. I lift his glass, dip the tip of my finger in, and make the three symbols as I visualize success.

"What's taking so long? What are you doing over there?"

"There was something floatin' in your glass, darlin'. I just wanted to get it out before I gave it to you." I hurry toward the couch and hand him his water.

Thankfully, he drinks deeply while I return for mine.

I pull out a chair at the table and sit down casually. "So, I think ya know my name's Daisy. What's your name?"

His eyes widen and his mouth struggles against opening, but fails. "Charles Sanderson."

"Hey, Charlie. Nice to meet you."

His horrified eyes blink.

I immediately press whatever advantage I might have. "So when are y'all gonna pull your next job?"

"Day after tomorrow."

"Well, isn't that nice. And what happens after that?"

He swallows and struggles to clench his jaw, all

to no avail. "Once we load everything into the two trucks, me and Jody have to drive them down to the meeting place at the warehouse in Chicago. We let the goods cool off, and then the boss arranges the fence."

"And what happens to me and my two friends?"

I can see Charlie struggling to hide the truth, but my extra senses pick up on something other than him fighting against the truth serum.

"Is something bad gonna happen to us?"

He nods. "He said no loose ends."

He doesn't need to draw me a picture. I'm pretty sure that means we all die. I'm not about to let that happen. Time to push that lack of trust in the gang to its limits. "Who makes the call? You said something about 'the boss,' but I thought you were in charge. You could just slip Denny his keys. We'll drive outta here and no one'll be the wiser. We're not gonna talk."

"Tibs took the gang from me." He points to the scar on his left cheek. "That's how I got this. He makes the calls now."

I hear wheels on the gravel outside. "Doesn't seem like your style, Charlie. You don't seem like the kinda man who would kill a little fella like Breck."

He swallows hard and shakes his head. "There's nothing I can do."

"There's always something, Charlie. There's always something."

Car doors slam.

I take my glass of water and walk toward the bedroom. "Tell you what, Charlie, you keep my secret about coming out for a glass of water, and I'll keep your secret about spilling the beans."

I hurry back into the room and shut the door.

CHAPTER 18

UNFORTUNATELY, Silas never taught me how to "deactivate" the truth runes. So about twenty minutes after I sneakily return to the bedroom, The Tank busts into the room and grabs me by the arm.

"My boy tells me you somehow got yourself out of a locked room. That's not the kind of thing that happens on my watch."

He drags me out of the room, through the kitchen, and outside.

For the first time since I got out of the trunk, I'm genuinely afraid for my life. I can feel the waves of anger rolling off The Tank.

He yanks my arm and pulls me around the cabin.

A small wooden outbuilding with a crescent moon painted on the door pops into view. There's something familiar about the symbol, but with my heart racing I can't quite place it.

He removes an unlocked padlock from a metal ring on the frame and flips the plate back.

We used to call that cowboy locked, back in Arizona. It means when you loop the chain, or hook a padlock, so that it appears secure to the casual passerby, but still allows easy access for those in the know.

As he opens the door, an unpleasant scent wafts toward my nostrils and I struggle to pull away as the meaning of the crescent moon symbol becomes all too clear.

"You should've thought about your options, girlie. We'll see what a couple days in here does for your sense of adventure."

He shoves me inside and slams the door behind.

I hear the distinct click of a padlock being locked—for real. As I survey my new tiny cage. My worst fears are confirmed.

I've just been locked inside a defunct outhouse. That means it hasn't been used in a very long time. However, that does not mean it doesn't smell! There's a rough-cut wooden box covering the toilet seat, but it is unsecured.

So, I guess the good news is that I have options.

A quick survey of the supplies at my disposal: half of an old, yellowed phone book, a completely empty toilet paper roll, and a large box of wooden matches with a grand total of seven remaining.

The real danger is that I'll die of dehydration long before the malodorous fumes render me unconscious.

Banging on the grey, reclaimed barn-wood door and screaming does nothing.

No one comes, and the construction, despite its age, is solid.

A quick attempt to rock the tiny prison off its foundation also proves fruitless. I sit down on the box and pout.

If I thought sleeping on a disco-era couch with no blanket was uncomfortable, sleeping in a tiny wooden outhouse, or long drop, should be downright horrifying.

At least I scarfed down some breakfast this morning.

I lean my head against the wooden wall behind me and stare at the vents on either side. Even if I succeed in knocking one of them loose, my bodacious hips will not allow me to escape through either of those portals. My only hope is that someone in the gang has a soft spot for damsels in distress and comes to deliver some food. I can knock them unconscious with this wooden box and make a run for it.

Barring that unlikely eventuality, it looks like

I'll be able to spend my time reflecting on my poor choices.

It might've been better to use my one escape opportunity to make a run for it, but I have no orienteering skills, and a run into the woods would've meant certain death. Had I stuck to the roads, the returning members of the gang would surely have seen me and dragged me back or worse—shot me on sight.

Maybe it's time to explore the limits of my psychic powers.

If I can communicate with Grams when I'm in the same room, maybe there's a way I can reach out to her from a great distance.

Perhaps Silas has some ability to snatch messages from the ether.

Or maybe my precious little Pyewacket has some sixth sense of his own and will feel that I'm in danger, in the same way that Lassie was always able to help Timmy out of the well.

First a return to the pity party for one.

I spend an indeterminate amount of time remembering all the wrong men in my life and far too little time wondering what would've happened if things had worked out with Erick and me.

Maybe I need to turn that frown upside down and say "when" things work out with Erick and me.

Seems like there's not much point in hoping for a psychic link up, if I've already accepted the worst.

I close my eyes, reach out with my senses and visualize connection, understanding, and rescue.

First with Grams, next with Silas, and finally with Pye.

The sun slips down so quickly that when I finish my exercise I'm surprised to find myself in utter blackness, blinking and waiting for moonrise.

I light a match and, for a moment, toy with the idea of burning my way free of the outhouse.

The most likely outcome of that plan would be that I would end up burning myself to death. Which seems like a horrible way to go.

Lighting another match, I watch as the flame burns down toward my thumb and finger, my sense of hope fading as the fire dies.

I tear a page from the phone book, roll it up tightly, and light the end. If I hold it straight up and down I'm hoping it will burn a little more slowly and keep the darkness at bay a moment longer.

As the flames reach my fingers, I drop the paper and stomp the fire out before my worst fears come true.

Silence and darkness weigh on me like a lead blanket.

Every insect that chirps, every leaf that ruffles

in the breeze, brings a chill to my skin and a pulse of adrenaline that sickens my stomach.

The moonlight has moved to the other set of louvers when I hear scratching on the wall of the outhouse. I clench my fists and shiver with fright.

My cover story and my secret Daisy identity are forgotten. I call out in a shaky voice, "Who is it? Who's there?"

"Ree-ow." A soft but condescending greeting.

I'm not sure if you've ever felt the hot and cold rush of ultimate relief mixed with renewed hope, but when I hear Pyewacket's all-too-familiar call, hot tears spill down my cheek. "Pye? Is it really you? Can you pick a padlock with your dew claw?"

A soft hiss. I'm not sure I've ever heard Pyewacket back down from a challenge before, but that reply seems as clear as day. He does not possess the skill to release me from my prison.

"Well, what's your plan? How did you find me?"

There's a light thud on the roof.

"Pyewacket?"

Claws scrape along the vent on the left side, followed by a low, motivating growl.

"All right, all right. I get it. This isn't the time to give up. I'm a smart girl. I can think of something." It feels good to talk to someone, or rather something. Mostly it feels good to not be alone. "Pye, here's what I've got: a few matches, half a telephone book, and a wooden box."

"RE-OW!" Game on!

The spark of encouragement from Pyewacket gives me an idea.

I'm so excited. I can't even remember what movie or TV show gave me this nugget. I take out a match, strike it and let it burn for a few seconds. Then I blow it out and start to scratch a message on one of the pages from the phone book with my little stick of charcoal.

After the first stroke, I stop.

I only have three matches left. I'm not sure how many words I'll be able to write per matchstick, so I better make a good plan before I compose my manifesto.

Clearly my location is the number one most valuable detail.

The number of captors is important.

The fact that Denny and Breck are here is also critical intel.

The jumble of letters begins to organize itself in my mind and I get to work. I can only see what I've previously written for the few seconds that I let each match burn. The writing is terrible, and very serial killer-y, but all I can do is hope against hope that Pyewacket can get this into the right hands and that those hands will be connected to a brain that can make heads or tails of my mess.

Two islands

Charlie Sanderson

6 robbers

Denny

Breck

heist tmrrw

Red pl—

The final match crumbles.

Looks like that's it. That's my message.

I fold the page several times and roll it as tight as I can. Then I poke it through the grate with a plea to my furry savior. "Pyewacket, you need to get this to Erick. Don't waste any time."

I feel his whiskers poke through the metal louvers as his teeth clamp onto my little tube of a message. He scratches the grating with his claws and I hear a soft thud as he hits the ground.

That's it. That's all my hope rolled up in a badly written communiqué, clenched in the mouth of a four-legged feline.

If you can hear me, Isadora, "I love you, Grams."

And now we wait.

CHAPTER 19

THE COLD, damp night air makes sleeping impossible. Not to mention the slap-fest that fills my little box once the mosquitoes discover me. I've heard folks in Pin Cherry joke about the "skeeters" being as big as birds. I no longer find that analogy amusing.

My new concern rapidly becomes dying from blood loss as these miniature, flying vampires drain me dry.

The blue-grey streaks of dawn finally defeat the endless night and I stretch my tired limbs.

Footsteps approach outside. I quickly scoop up my burned matchstick crumbs, lift the wooden box, and dump the evidence into the latrine. I manage to get the box back in place over the hole and take a seat before the door opens.

The Tank stands outside with a frustrated scowl pinching his features.

Digging deep to muster up "Daisy," I smile and say, "Mornin' boss."

He sniffs and frowns. "The boys said you made good eggs."

I believe that's his way of inviting me to come back inside and make breakfast. "Happy to help."

Daisy might be happy. Mitzy is furious. But if the only way to keep myself out of that smelly wooden torture box is to be useful . . . I can be very useful.

The Tank pushes me through the front door toward the serviceable kitchen. I swallow my protest of the rough treatment and gather supplies.

A quick glance toward the couch confirms that Denny and Breck are still alive and well.

I make a lot of noise, while purposely moving at a snail's pace. I plan to stretch out this meal prep as long as possible, and maybe shove some bacon in my pockets for later.

When the first pot of coffee finishes brewing, I make the rounds, Tally-style, and fill each of the six mugs at the table. Once I serve the gang, I take another mug from the cupboard, fill it with coffee, and turn toward the couch. "Do you take anything in your coffee, Denny?"

Ponytail chuckles. "Yeah, Denny. You take any-thing in your coffee?"

Three of the crew snicker.

The hair on the back of my neck tingles, but no additional information is forthcoming. I take a chance and walk the cup of coffee over to Denny.

"Can I get you some water, Breck?"

The little boy nods his tear-stained face and I return to the kitchen to flip the bacon and fill a water glass.

The Tank leans back in his chair. "What's taking so long, Daisy?"

"Sorry, darlin'. Guess I'm just moving slower than a pregnant snappin' turtle. Runnin' on no sleep and all."

I hear Scarface grumble something under his breath and Ponytail punches him in the arm.

Not that I care what's said. I just want to stir up a little trouble in the ranks and possibly guilt trip The Tank into keeping me inside tonight.

Transferring the bacon to a plate, I quickly scramble up the eggs. As usual, The Tank receives the first serving, then the rest of the gang, and then I take a plate piled for two over to Denny.

Once again, no one protests. So when I return to the kitchen, I fill my own plate and wolf down two strips of bacon and a pile of eggs before any-one's the wiser.

The Tank looks up. "You sure don't eat like a lady. And there better be seconds for me."

Guilt washes over me as I realize how my hunger pains erased all residue of Daisy and replaced her with ravenous Mitzy. Time to simmer back down and throw on the southern charm. "I saved the best bit for you."

Scarface leans back and smirks. "You hear that, Tibs, she's playing favorites."

After I refill The Tank's plate, I set it down and smile. "Tibs. Is that short for Thibodeau? I had an uncle named Thibodeau."

The Tank reaches out with his huge mitt and clamps it around my wrist. "No names."

"Just makin' conversation."

He releases my wrist and tucks into his second breakfast.

Making another pot of coffee, I manage a half-cup for myself.

The chore of cleaning up after breakfast easily buys me some additional time outside the hot box.

Ponytail comes storming out of the bathroom with nothing but a towel wrapped around his waist.

Mitzy stares for a little too long at the chiseled abs and multiple tattoos, before Daisy reminds her to act like a lady. Talking to ghosts and herding a wildcat is simple, compared to managing two personalities in one body.

He points accusingly at Denny as he addresses The Tank. "You said you were going to send him into town with some laundry. I got no clean clothes and I'm sick of sharing a towel with five other guys."

The Tank stands up real slow and cracks his knuckles.

Time to prevent Breck from witnessing any more violence. "I'd be happy to scrub them clothes. I can wash 'em here in the sink and hang 'em on a line outside. They'll be dry in two shakes of a lamb's tail. No trouble at all."

The Tank looks at me and nods his head. "You heard Daisy, boys. Pile your laundry in the kitchen. She's looking to make herself useful."

I shudder to think how raw my knuckles will be after scrubbing all those clothes in the kitchen sink, but I'm honestly looking forward to using that scrub brush on my mosquito bites! The mere thought of them causes a flare up. I scratch viciously at my left arm.

Denny glances across the room. "Skeeters?"

I nod and whimper.

"Boil some water, stick a spoon in it for thirty seconds. Press the hot spoon on the mosquito bite as long as you can stand it. Does something to the poison. Can't really explain it, but it'll stop itching."

Filling a pot with water, I set it on the stove, as the gang piles their laundry on the kitchen table. I run a sink full of warm sudsy water, and wait for the pot on the stove to come to a boil.

When I hear the bubbling, I turn and run smack dab into the imposing form of The Tank.

He grabs my arm. "You can deal with your bug bites after these clothes are on the line."

A little mind-montage clouds my vision. A knee to the groin. Two hands behind his bald head that smash his nose onto the other knee. Elbow to the back of the neck. The sound of him hitting the floor. Ah, yes. Just running through the scenario in my brain relieves some of the stress of holding it all in. "You're the boss."

I hear Charlie scoff under his breath as he rubs the scar on his left cheek.

The Tank instantly drops my arm and leans menacingly toward Charlie, a.k.a. Scarface. "You got something to say to me?"

"Course not. You're in charge. You wanna run a job and juggle hostages, that's your call, Bossman. I prefer plans with simple payoffs and less baggage."

The Tank reaches across the table, grabs a fistful of Charlie's shirt, and yanks him forward. "It's my plans that got us the big jobs. My plans that paid for the trucks. Don't you forget it." He releases Scarface with a shove and storms out the front door of the cabin.

As the screen door slams home, an uncomfortable silence hangs in the air.

I pick some of the smallclothes from the table and toss them into the water to soak.

"I agree with you, Charlie. It don't make no sense to take such a risk right on the heels of y'all's last job."

Charlie smooths his shirt and shakes his head. "It's unpredictable. Cops don't expect it. That's why we never get caught."

Grabbing a pair of jeans off the table, I gaze heavenward. "From your mouth to God's ears, Charlie."

I turn around and surreptitiously search the pockets before I toss the jeans into the sink.

The pile of dirty clothes dwindles as the pile of slightly cleaner clothes grows. After a thorough search of the shirt and pants pockets of the various items I'm cleaning for the gang, I come up with loose change, which I lay on the table to demonstrate my honesty, and a business card for a storage facility in Chicago, which I shove into my bra.

"Hey y'all, I finished the washing. Who gets to watch me hang it outside?"

Scarface gets up from the table and walks over to Ponytail. He holds out his hand. "Gimme the gun."

Surprisingly, Ponytail hands his gun over without argument.

"Let's go, Daisy. Grab that laundry."

"Yes, sir." I pick up the bundle of wet laundry and feel a flash of gratitude that my tank top is black, and not a terrible, see-through-when-wet color like white.

Outside we find some rope in a shed and string up a temporary clothesline between two trees. I drape the laundry over the line as best I can. The cord stretches some under the weight of the wet clothes, but the gentle breeze and the warm sunshine should soon fix that problem.

"What'd you decide, Charlie?"

"About what?"

"'Bout saving that little boy." I shake out another pair of jeans and drape them over a low hanging branch.

His voice is barely a whisper. "You know the story, Daisy. And I told you, Tibs makes all the decisions."

I shake out the last towel and hang it over what remains of the clothesline. "Seems like an awful thing to have on your conscience though, Charlie. That little boy didn't hurt nobody. Why don't you give me Denny's keys and I'll make sure Breck gets outta here safely."

I sense a shift in Charlie's energy and I feel like I might be getting through to him.

As he looks up his face goes from understanding to ashen in a moment.

I spin around.

The Tank grabs me by the arm and drags me toward the outhouse. "Looks like you earned yourself another night in the box, girlie. I run this crew. I make these men a lot of money. They're not gonna turn on me for a skirt." He twists my arm a little harder for emphasis. "You might want to think about saving your own skin before you waste time and energy on a kid you don't know from Adam."

My desperation is growing by leaps and bounds, and I have no way of knowing if my secret message ever made it to Erick. No rescue showed up at our doorstep so far today, so I have to start playing for keeps. Maybe I can't save everyone. But I believe in my heart I can save Breck.

As The Tank starts to close the outhouse door, I lean against it desperately. "Did Denny tell you he kidnapped that kid from his ex-wife before he headed up here?"

I'm not even sure if I stayed in character for that line. But the look on The Tank's face is worth it.

"You give me that kid and a set of keys and I can take the heat off you. Think about it."

He shoves me backward, slams the outhouse door, and the padlock clicks.

At least I know I won't be the only one *not* getting any sleep tonight.

CHAPTER 20

THE DISTINCT ODOR of cigarette smoke awakens me from my uncomfortable moment of seated slumber.

"Pssst. Daisy, up here."

As I look up, a piece of bacon jabs through the vents.

I reach and grab it without hesitation. "Thanks, Charlie."

"Daisy? What happened to your accent?"

With my mouth full of bacon, it's a little hard to reply. Which gives me a moment to decide exactly what I want to say.

Truth time.

"It hardly seems important now. My name isn't Daisy and I don't have a southern accent. And since

I'm apparently going to die in an outhouse, I guess I don't really care anymore, Charlie."

There's a low chuckle.

"What's so funny?"

"If it was up to me, I'd say we could use a girl like you on our crew." He coughs and stamps out his cigarette. "But it's not. Sorry about all this. Gotta go."

Pounding my fist on the wood, I shout, "I could be on the crew . . ."

No reply.

So much for turning to a life of crime to avoid death.

Raised voices from inside the cabin reach my ear and I wonder if my smoke-pit buddy is arguing to save me or if Denny is arguing to save his son.

Either way, this has turned out to be one of my worst ideas ever.

Loud voices escalate to screaming and shouting.

A gunshot.

Silence.

I press my ear to the door of the outhouse and listen.

The front door slams several times.

Three engines start.

Two vehicles speed away.

The front door slams one final time.

The last vehicle tears down the gravel road, rocks pinging off metal. Everything falls quiet.

Even the birds are silent.

Wait, is someone smoking? I definitely smell smoke. It's different than cigarette—

Sobs followed by Breck's frightened voice screaming, "Daddy! Daddy!" tell me everything I need to know.

Those jerks must've shot Denny and then set the cabin on fire.

I sit down on the wooden box, lean back, and bring my knees to my chest. Shouting like a judo master, I repeatedly kick the rough-hewn wooden door with full force.

Finally, the third blow cracks some of the boards.

Two more donkey kicks and I've created a hole big enough to squeeze through. My wig catches on the splintered boards and rips off my head despite the bobby pins.

I race toward the front door. It's fully engulfed in flames. Running back to the outhouse, I grab a splintered board from the ground and scream through the closed bedroom window, "Breck, get back from the window!"

Taking the board, I smash out the glass, scraping carefully to get all the broken shards from the bottom of the frame.

Digging my toes into the split-rock foundation and grabbing onto the warped window ledge, I scramble up and fall into the room.

Smoke is roiling under the door.

Denny is motionless.

Breck is frantic.

"Breck, you climb out that window. I'll get your dad."

He looks up at my wild white hair with tears streaming down his sooty face. "Who are you? Are you an angel? Am I dead?"

"Not if I can help it." I pick him up and gently push him through the window. It's quite a drop, but a possible broken bone is definitely better than staying in this flaming cabin.

The smoke and heat are starting to scorch my lungs, and Denny is a big guy. I grab a pillowcase off the bed and tie it around my face.

Hooking my arms under his armpits, I focus on summoning the same strength I found when I broke out of my wooden prison.

I drag Denny toward the window as the pool of dark red on his shirt spreads.

I look away.

I can't afford to pass out right now.

As I bend and regrip, he mumbles, "Breck?"

"He's outside. You have to climb out this window, Denny. Please, if you have any strength, help me get you out of here."

He struggles to get his feet underneath him. But he's so weak and his wound looks horrible. "Leave me," he mumbles.

I lean his head and shoulders out the window. "Push with your legs."

He tries, but he's stuck halfway, like a teeter-totter.

Coughing as more thick smoke billows into the room, I can hear the flames crackling outside the bedroom door.

Scooping my arms around his legs, I lift and shove.

He dumps out of the window headfirst.

I dive out after him.

"Breck, I need your help, all right?"

He stares at me and nods, as sobs shake his body.

"You get down by the lake. Down by the dock. All right?"

"What about my dad?" Tears run down his cheeks and snot leaks from his nose.

"I'll bring your dad. Just get down to the lake."

He turns and runs as orange flames lick around the sides of the log cabin. Smoke heaves into the sky and, once again, I scoop my arms under Denny and use all of my remaining strength to drag him toward the small dock.

Hopefully, the birch and pine trees around the cabin are trimmed back far enough to prevent the fire from spreading to the forest. I don't think I have enough energy left to drag the old wooden boat down by myself. The rack is nearly a foot above my head.

For a moment, a flash of memory distracts me. Didn't Denny say he brought Breck up here to teach him how to fish? But then he said the boat was probably leaky and he didn't have gas for the engine. I look at the black cloud swirling in my mood ring and receive no magical footnote to my random thoughts.

Better focus on surviving the current dilemma rather than Denny's half-truths.

I'll keep my fingers crossed that the flames draw enough attention to bring assistance before time runs out for him.

Pulling the pillowcase off my face, I shove it on his bullet wound and apply pressure. I have no medical training, but, in the movies, they always apply pressure.

Breck's sitting on the dock sobbing quietly, but he's alive.

At least I kept one promise.

As I continue to apply pressure the pillowcase reddens and Denny reaches weakly for my arm.

"They double-crossed me."

"What?" When his fingers clutch me, a series of images, feelings, and knowings wash over me.

The psychic barrage leaves me breathless. "You were working with them?"

"Needed the cash. Save Breck."

"How did you link up with them? They tried to kill you and your son. How could you trust a gang of lowlifes like that?"

"Sanderson. Army."

"Charlie? You and Charlie served together?" Of all the names I could've written on that secret note . . . Pyewacket, please tell me you got that note to Erick!

His head nods and he moans in pain.

"Daddy?" Breck takes a hesitant step toward us.

"You stay down by the water, Breck. Help is on the way and your dad needs to focus on breathing."

Denny's hand slips off my arm and thuds onto the ground.

I lean down and hiss into his ear, "Don't you dare take the easy way out, Denny. You better live long enough to apologize to Karen and make sure your son doesn't turn out like you."

There's no reply.

CHAPTER 21

My throat burns, my mouth tastes like soot, and my arms are numb with exhaustion.

When I hear the chorus of sirens it feels like a dream.

I'm so relieved the smoke brought us rescuers, I don't even have time to be annoyed that the first one on the scene is Deputy Paulsen.

"Moon? What are you doing up here at the McMurray's cabin?"

I opt to skip my usual banter with my least favorite deputy. "He's been shot in the gut. I've been applying pressure."

She yells over her shoulder and another deputy appears. "Help me get this guy in my cruiser. There's no time to wait for an ambulance."

The other officer grabs Denny's shoulders, while she takes his feet.

I try to keep applying pressure as they move.

Paulsen looks at me. "He's not gonna make it, Moon. Go back and get the kid." She breaks eye contact and adds, "You did a good thing—rescuing that kid. Make sure he gets back to his mom in one piece."

Her out-of-character kind words leave me speechless. I move my head in a slow up and down motion and pull my hands away from the blood-soaked pillowcase.

She glances at Denny. "I hate to say it, but this guy got what he deserves."

A huge lump rises in my throat. "This guy" may be guilty of kidnapping his own son and abusing his wife, but I'm not sure he deserved to go out like this. I still can't find any words. I wring my hands and stare.

She jerks her head toward the lake. "The kid."

I swallow the lump and try to put on a brave face for Breck.

Jogging back toward the broken little boy, I rinse my hands in the lake before I approach him.

His breathing is ragged and tears sluice down his small cheeks.

I crouch and place a comforting hand on his

shoulder. "Let's get you back to your mom. All right?"

His wide, innocent eyes stare up at me with awe. "I prayed you'd save us."

I have no words.

Scooping him into my arms, I run toward the second cruiser.

Paulsen has already peeled away with Denny. Despite her sour outlook, I admire that she's making every effort to get him medical attention.

The deputy who stayed behind, motions for us to get in the back of his vehicle.

"Hey, would you like to ride in a police car with me?"

Breck nods.

Sliding the boy into the vehicle, I drop onto the bench seat next to him.

As the adrenaline dissipates, the mosquito bites come itching back with a vengeance.

The deputy gets in and hits the lights and sirens.

Despite the days of trauma this little boy has endured he looks up at me and smiles. "It's just like in the movies."

I ruffle his dark hair and force a smile. "Exactly."

Leaning forward, I grip the wire grate separating us from the officer. "Deputy, my name's

Mitzy Moon and this is Breck Jordan. I believe his mother's looking for him."

"Yes, ma'am. And half the town's been looking for you as well."

Embarrassing and heartwarming news. "You should probably call it in then."

He fumbles with his radio. "Right. Only been on the job a few months. Never thought a small town would see so much action. Still, wish I coulda been on the task force."

That sounds like an interesting story, but it'll wait until we get this little guy safely into his mother's arms.

Deputy Michelson, as I hear him introduce himself over the radio, calls in the safe recovery of the missing persons Mitzy Moon and Breck Jordan as we speed toward Pin Cherry.

When we pull up in front of the Birch County Regional Medical Facility, I see my dad's pickup truck and Silas's ridiculous Model T parked near the Emergency entrance.

After believing I was an orphan for more than a decade, I can't tell you how much it means to have someone waiting for me—to have people.

I've got people.

The cruiser barely makes it to a stop before Karen races out of the ER with tears streaming down her face.

I attempt to open the car door, but the backseats of cop cars aren't built for prisoner's selective exit. No door handle on the inside. I lift my hands and signal to the distraught woman.

She yanks the door open and Breck climbs over me to launch himself into her arms.

She hugs him so tight. I can feel her gratitude in my soul.

The medical professionals swoop in and transfer him to a gurney.

Karen runs beside the bed, holding Breck's hand as they hurry inside.

A wave of longing for my own mother hits me in the gut. I'll never hold her hand again.

This day is going to destroy me.

Before I have a chance to sink into an emotional puddle of nostalgia, my dad runs out and scoops me into his arms.

He rubs a thumb across my face and smiles. "Did you get a job as a coal miner?"

I laugh uncontrollably. Filled with relief and love and exhaustion. I peek around my father's broad shoulders hoping to see Erick, but I'm equally pleased to see Silas quietly shuffling toward us.

"It would appear that once again, that uncanny feline has saved your life."

Jacob releases me and I throw my arms around Silas and his frumpy tweed coat, inhaling the aromas of pipe smoke and denture cream as though they were chocolate mousse and pin cherry pie.

"I used a few tricks you taught me, too. A little alchemy comes in handy in a pinch."

Silas hugs me back and his jowls shake as he chuckles.

Deputy Michelson exchanges information with a nurse, but there's still no sign of Erick.

I turn to my father, but before I can ask my burning question, he says, "He's on a secret mission."

"Who?"

My father shakes his head. "The man you keep looking for. I told him about your elaborate plan to load a boxcar with dummy merchandise and run some kind of sting operation. Next thing I know, he's telling me how Paulsen's gonna have to check the cabins on his list because he's leading the SWAT team that's planning to take down the train robbers."

All the happiness drains out of my heart, and in its place I feel a horrible ache of impending doom. "What? Why can't he just let the FBI handle things? Why does he keep putting himself in danger?"

My father holds me at arm's length and stares. "Have you looked in the mirror lately?"

I lift my arm to give my dad a playful punch on

the arm, but everything goes sideways, and when I open my eyes, there's a cannula pushing oxygen through my nasal passages and an IV urging fluids into my vein.

"Good afternoon, Mitzy." Silas smiles at me. "Your father went to retrieve some coffee. He'll be pleased to see you've chosen to grace us—"

Jacob walks into the room, sees my eyes open, and immediately sloshes the coffees onto the bedside table. He bends and kisses my forehead. "I feel like I'm always telling you to stop scaring the daylights out of me, but at the risk of repeating myself— don't ever do that again!"

"Copy that." The electrolytes in the IV are working their magic and I feel almost normal. "When can I get out of here?"

My father shakes his head. "Where do you need to be?"

I'm torn between racing to the bookshop to make sure Grams knows I'm all right, and staking out the sheriff's station so I can be the first one to see Erick—alive and kicking.

"Before you make any long-term arrangements, you will be required to make a full statement. Deputy Michelson asked that I convey you to the station after your release."

I roll my eyes. "Fine. Somebody"—I look at my father and give him my best puppy-dog eyes—"get my discharge paperwork started, and I'm going to check on Breck."

While I attempt to push the right combination of buttons to elevate the head of my bed, I pull the tube out of my nose, throw my blankets back, swing my legs over the side, and stare at the IV in my left hand. My right hand hovers above the tape and gauze.

Jacob grips my hand firmly. "I don't know what scene from what movie you're playing in your mind right now, but it hurts like heck to pull out an IV needle. You roll this little rack along with you to Breck's room and I'll get your paperwork handled. Deal?"

I'm not that into pain, but I don't want to seem like a pushover. "Fine. Have it your way." I grab my little rolling IV cart with my left hand and toddle out of my room. I smile when I imagine what a classic scene I must make.

The nurse at the desk is so nice and helpful that it sends me into a momentary panic. What if I'm dying? What if everyone is just being nice to the poor girl with the burned up lungs?

I stop in the hallway, grip the safety railing bolted to the faded green wall with my right hand, and take two deep breaths. Nothing bursts. I don't faint. I'm still alive.

All right. I may have overreacted.

By the time I reach the pediatrics wing, I'm wishing I'd put on pants. Thankfully, I'm only one of many wanderers wearing the hospital's pale floral print and no one gives me a second glance.

The door to Breck's room is closed and there's a doctor inside, whispering close to Karen. I toy with the idea of reaching out with my psychic senses to see if I can hear what he's saying, but I'm concerned about the effect that could have on my recovery. Instead, I opt for a knock.

Karen's gaze snaps to the door, but when she sees me, the strain evaporates and a weary smile touches her lips. She gestures for me to come in.

The doctor eyes me with concern.

"This is the woman who saved my son, doctor." Karen rushes over and hugs me, careful to avoid my medical apparatus.

The doctor nods. "Breck is lucky you got him out. Other than bumps and bruises, he's in great shape." He takes a tablet off a stand and tucks it under his arm. "I'll return to check his vitals in three hours."

"Thank you, doctor."

He leaves, and Karen pushes a chair toward me and scoots one over for herself.

I manage to scrape my unwieldy IV cart into position beside me and lower myself onto the chair.

Karen grips my right hand. "I had a whole

speech planned, but the doctor just told me that Denny didn't make it—so, I'm kind of a wreck."

As soon as she mentions Denny, I glance at Breck. He looks like he's sound asleep, and I wonder how he'll manage this terrible news on top of all the awful things he's already endured. "I'm sorry, Karen. I tried—"

She rubs my hand. "Don't say another word. Denny had options. He had people who loved him and wanted to help him. He shut himself off from everything that was good in his life. I couldn't reach him anymore." She shakes her head as if it will erase the bad memories. "I will never stop loving him and I'll never say a bad word against him in front of Breck."

My extrasensory perception picks up on what she's not saying. She's relieved. And she's riddled with guilt because of it. "My Grams always used to say, 'one day at a time.' That's all you can manage, Karen. Just be there for Breck. He's going to need to process all of this. Those guys were not good guys. They shot Denny in front of Breck."

Karen gasps.

"I'm not saying it to cause you more pain. But I thought you should know."

She nods, and her red eyes seem unable to produce any more tears. "Breck is special. He believes in redemption," she whispers.

I nod and rub her back. "When I broke into the room to get him, he thought I was an angel."

She looks at me and my heart swells with the love I feel emanating from her. "When I tell this story—the good parts, anyway—you'll always be an angel."

I sniffle and smile. "For what it's worth, I'm pretty sure Denny got shot trying to escape with Breck." I have no idea if it's true, but there's nothing to be gained by dragging a dead man through the mud.

"I appreciate you saying that. I'll try to help Breck re-frame things, but I'll never know what really happened. I can't imagine how worried Denny must've been when that gang commandeered the cabin."

I swallow hard. She doesn't know about Charlie or the deal Denny made to try and get cash for a life on the run. Hopefully, it will never come out, now that Denny's crossed over. I don't know why, but the mention of crossing over suddenly makes me think of Ghost-ma. "I've got to get home, Karen. I hope we meet again, under better circumstances." I gather up all my tubing and my little IV pole and get to my feet.

Karen walks me to the door and puts a gentle hand on my arm. "It's probably none of my business, but when you ran out of the sheriff's station after you saw Erick comforting me, he was gutted. I've known him a long time. He's never cared about anything as much as he seems to care about you." She squeezes my arm. "I hope you'll give him another chance."

Three days ago I would've told her to mind her own business, but after everything I've been through, my heart is feeling a little more open to the kindness of strangers. I pat her hand and smile—the real kind of smile that touches my eyes and hopefully her heart. "Thanks for the tip. Let me know if you or Breck ever need anything."

She returns my smile and walks back toward her son.

Time for me to get to the bookshop. Grams must be going crazy.

CHAPTER 22

TRUE TO HIS WORD, my father uses the weight of the "Duncan" name to secure my early discharge, in spite of the protests of my medical retinue.

Changing out of my hospital finery and into my sweaty, sooty, hostage clothes is less than appealing, and I beg my attorney for some "me" time before he drags me down to the station to make my official statement.

Silas promises to keep Deputy Michelson at bay long enough for me to handle my personal hygiene, as well as my ghost business, and Jacob drives me home.

He drops me off right in front of the bookshop and offers to walk me in.

"It's all right, Dad. I feel like a new woman after

all the electrolytes and whatever else was in that IV. I can handle Grams on my own."

"I'm not worried about you wrangling Mom. I want to make sure you walk straight into that building without getting yourself into any more trouble!" He enjoys a snicker at my expense.

Leaning into the window of his old truck, I quip, "To steal a line from Grams, 'Well, I never!'"

He winks. "Take care, kid."

I'd love to say I sprint into my wonderful bookstore, but recovering from dehydration, smoke inhalation, and exhaustion translates into more of a limping hobble. Maybe I wasn't completely honest with my dad about the whole "new woman" nonsense. However, I manage to keep up a steady shamble.

The bookshop is open, and as I walk in I hear a surprising number of voices among the stacks. When I round the corner, their queen bee turns and leads them all in a standing ovation.

"There she is, folks. Local hero Mitzy Moon, owner of the Bell, Book & Candle." Twiggy hands me the "Special Edition" of the *Pin Cherry Harbor Post*. "Made the front page again, doll."

Only in a town this small could a midday "Special Edition" be put together on such short notice. I mutely take the offered copy and stare wordlessly at the photos above the fold. The black-and-white image of Karen cradling her rescued son is everything. Where was Quince Knudsen? I don't remember seeing him at the hospital. He must've heard the call come in over his police scanner and raced to the ER. That kid has an undeniable talent for capturing truth.

"How 'bout that one of you and Jacob?" Twiggy turns to her audience. "That's one for the scrapbooks. Right, ladies?"

As they continue to offer praise and pose questions, I gaze at the image of my dad and me. Quince captured the exact moment when Jacob rubbed his thumb across my cheek and made his joke about coal miners. Every time I see this, I know I'll feel the exact rush of relief and unconditional love that flooded through me right then.

My dad and I have a habit of making jokes to cover our deeper feelings, but thanks to my extra senses, my heart overflowed with the bond of family as he and I were reunited. I see why people say an image like that is priceless. However, knowing Quince as a teen that takes cash seriously, I'm pretty sure I'll be able to put a price on that negative that he'll accept.

Twiggy leads her minions in a chant of, "Speech! Speech! Speech!"

I take one look at the coffee klatch that she's assembled, unhook the "No Admittance" chain, and drag myself upstairs to the apartment.

When the bookcase slides open Grams hits me with a full head of steam.

"Mitzy! You look a fright! Get yourself in the shower, and I'll choose an outfit for your press conference."

The tiredness has seeped into my bones and I can't find the energy to ask or argue. I put one foot in front of the other, peeling off my filthy clothes as I go.

Staying in the shower all day sounds like a completely plausible option. I never thought it could feel so good to be clean. I utterly lose track of time as steam surrounds me and eucalyptus shampoo tingles my scalp. This is the life.

Eventually, my curiosity about Erick's mission resurfaces and I shut off the glorious steaming water.

With my head swaddled in a turban and a second towel luxuriously wrapped around my person, I stumble into my couture closet to see what Grams has selected.

"Look, I need to sleep for like a week. What on earth are you dressing me for?"

"First and foremost, I want you to look your best when you're reunited with Erick. And second of all, I'm sure that young man you know from the newspaper will want to take a picture when they hear about your heroic efforts to break up the Stopwatch Robbers."

"Too late on that second one, Grams. Somehow Quince managed to grab his award-winning photos in front of the hospital's ER entrance. Twiggy is showing off the 'Special Edition' images to a gaggle of groupies down in the stacks."

She stops and I can almost see the wheels turning in her ethereal head. "Well, no point crying over spilt milk! We can still make the reunion picture-perfect." She resumes her search for the outfit that will save my floundering relationship.

"When you say reunited with Erick, did you have one of your afterlife clairvoyant visions that assures me his mission will be successful?"

Her shimmering eyes avoid mine.

"Grams, was that just wishful thinking?"

"I don't know about any secret mission. Remember? No one tells the ghost anything! I'm referring to your budding romance. It pays to be positive, Mitzy. Maybe you need to recite the Serenity Prayer."

While Grams flits around my closet hemming and hawing over options, I slip on a familiar pair of skinny jeans and one of my old T-shirts. This has a picture of the solar system and says, "Back in my day, we had nine planets."

I head into the bathroom, fix my face with a minimal amount of effort, and run my fingers through my damp hair.

The crumpled business card on the pile of my discarded underthings grabs my attention. I retrieve it and slip it into my bra for an imagined dramatic reveal later. When—not if—I see Erick.

Without a word, I leave the apartment before Grams can protest.

Down on the first floor Twiggy and her groupies are nowhere to be seen. Muffled cackles come from somewhere, though. They must have moved into the museum area, and I gladly slip out the front door unnoticed.

The warm sunshine and the feeling of freedom re-energize my depleted ch'i. Oh, if the folks back in Sedona could hear me now!

Silas is kindly waiting at the sheriff's station when I arrive and informs me that my father was needed at the depot.

"No problem. I just thought I should come in and make a statement."

Silas approaches Deputy Baird, a.k.a. Furious Monkeys, and she waves Michelson over to take my statement.

"Follow me into Interrogation Room Two. We'll have a little more privacy there."

Searching the station, I don't see any sign of Erick.

Deputy Michelson motions Silas and me to the uncomfortable chairs on one side of the table and closes the door. He sits opposite us and clicks on the recording device. "Deputy Michelson taking an official statement from—" He looks at me and nods, but before I can answer Silas interjects, "Mizithra Achelois Moon."

I roll my eyes. "Mitzy Moon will be fine."

I tell my tale, beginning with my official recruitment to the confidential informant program and ending with the fire at the cabin.

"And how did you get out of the, um, outhouse?"

"I guess it was one of those fear-induced adrenaline things. When I smelled the smoke and realized Breck was trapped inside the cabin, I just kicked the door down somehow."

"There's one thing I don't understand." He rubs his thumb along his lightly freckled cheek.

"And what's that, Deputy?"

"We were already headed that way when we saw the smoke. How did Deputy Paulsen know where to find you?"

I glance at Silas, hoping for some indication as to whether or not I should share what I suspect about Pyewacket's involvement.

Silas leans forward. "I believe Deputy Paulsen received a tip from Sheriff Harper as to the possible location of the hostages."

Silas for the win. He may look like a doddering old man, but inside his neurons are firing lightning fast.

"Is there anything you'd like to add to your statement, Miss Moon?"

"Not at this time, Deputy." I make no mention of Denny's deathbed confessions. Those details hardly seem important—now.

A commotion out front brings Deputy Michelson to his feet. He puts a hesitant hand on his gun and opens the door slowly. He peers out, and as his shoulders physically relax I sense his anxiety evaporate.

He turns toward Silas and me. "Looks like they were successful."

I jump to my feet. If "they were successful" means Erick is back alive, I'm all over this.

Shoving past him, I burst into the bullpen, just as Scarface, Ponytail, The Tank, and the three guys I didn't have time to nickname are escorted into the station in handcuffs. A bunch of super-tough looking dudes in Kevlar vests, helmets, and strapped up to the hilt are bringing up the rear. For those of you who haven't watched a ton of gangster movies like me, "strapped up" means equipped with a lot of guns.

Scanning the faces of the law enforcement professionals manhandling the criminals I search for Erick, but no joy.

One of the men, who's probably with the FBI, leans over the counter and passes some information to Deputy Baird.

I quietly reach out with my extrasensory perception and hear him mention something about two wounded officers.

Without thinking, I rush forward.

Some over-reactive guy in Kevlar intercepts me, whips my arms behind my back, and clicks me in handcuffs before I make it three strides.

I'm about to shout a classic "do you know who I am" line when the front door opens and a pair of anxious blue eyes lock onto me.

He rushes forward and shoves the SWAT guy off me. "Back off, Cleveland. That's my CI." Erick unhooks one of my handcuffs, spins me around, and plants a huge kiss on my speechless lips.

No matter what else happens, this will always be the best day of my life.

CHAPTER 23

You know that scene in the movie when the lead actor scoops the lead actress into his arms and carries her off-screen to what you know is going to be their happily-ever-after? In real life, things are never quite that flawless.

When Erick finally comes up for air, there is no round of applause or fade to black.

Instead, Cleveland smacks Erick on the back and says, "I guess you guys handle your CIs a little differently up north!"

The room erupts in laughter.

Heat rises up my freshly scrubbed cheeks and I step back awkwardly.

Erick appears to have a similar flood of self-consciousness and becomes urgently occupied with unhooking his Kevlar vest.

The man I saw leaning over the counter talking to Furious Monkeys approaches and puts a fatherly hand on Erick's shoulder. "We'll take it from here, Sheriff. Why don't you get changed and debrief your CI."

I'm not sure why that phrase fills me with tingles. But now my cheeks are certainly a shade of fuchsia only seen in comic books.

I attempt to shuffle past Erick toward escape, but we bump into one another awkwardly. "I was—"

He coughs. "Maybe just—"

"Myrtle's?" I mumble.

He holds his breath and nods, as he dives to the left and hustles toward his office.

I salute the FBI guy officially and hurry toward the exit with my proverbial tail between my legs.

However, a step from the door my mood ring heats up and I look down in time to see a business card. A smug grin graces my face and I circle back to the room full of testosterone. "Hey, G-man."

The fatherly FBI agent turns and cocks his head in a far too patronizing manner. "What's up, Miss?"

I reach into my bra, extract the card, and fan it back and forth. I had hoped to play this scene out with Erick, but I think this will tip the scales back in his favor with the Feds. "You might want to dispatch an agent to collect the stash of stolen goods from this location."

His expression immediately shifts to suspicious interest. He strides forward and takes the card. "Where did you get this?"

"Oh, that's confidential." I nod my head. "That's how we CIs do it up north."

The bullpen ripples with laughter and locker room gibes.

Time for me to skedaddle, before I ruin this perfect take.

For once in this small town, I make it to the diner ahead of the "news." For at least fifteen glorious minutes, I enjoy my burger and fries in blessed silence.

But miracles are only meant for saints, so when Odell saunters out from behind the grill, I know my number is up.

He slides across the squeaky-clean red vinyl covering the bench seat opposite me and folds his hands in his lap. "Now, I know I'm no relation, but I think Isadora would be disappointed if I didn't at least consider myself a surrogate grandfather."

I stare across the table at my grandmother's first husband and smile. "I think you're right."

"Well then, in that capacity, I'd like to say, you need to simmer down. You could've been the one getting carted away in a hearse today. An interstate train robbery gang? I can't believe even you were that careless. Your grandmother did some foolish things in her day, but she kept her head on a swivel. You've got to be more careful. There are people in this town who rely on you." He takes a napkin and rubs at a nonexistent smudge on the table.

"Rely on me? I'm not sure that's true."

"I can tell you right now, it would certainly hurt my french fry sales if you weren't around." He grins and raps his knuckles on the table as he exits the booth.

"Since you've got me on the free burgers and fries for life plan, seems like that would actually add to your bottom line."

He leans in and puts a hand on my shoulder. "Don't you worry about me. You've got your hands full keeping yourself alive."

"Copy that."

He walks away shaking his head, stops, and looks back. "Oh, I pretty near forgot. You got a minute?"

A glance toward the entrance reveals no sign of Erick. So, I smile and slide out of the booth. "For you? Always."

He gestures for me to follow him into the back. As we round the corner, I see some bright, shiny new metal wedged between the ancient grill and the equally archaic refrigerator.

Odell points to the new fryer and shrugs. "So, what do you know about this?"

Attempting to paint my features as the portrait of innocence, I reply, "Looks like a fryer. That's about all I can tell you."

He makes a sound that reminds me of the frustrated harrumph of Silas. "That so? No idea who paid for it or how it got here?"

I'm not prepared to tell an outright lie, so I attempt to carefully sidestep. "There are plenty of explanations."

He chuckles and crosses his arms over his smudged apron. "Do any of those explanations make a pit stop anywhere near the truth?"

I laugh and throw my hands up in the air like it's a stick-up. "All right, you got me. The Duncan-Moon Foundation has a certain amount of money set aside for community improvements and renovations."

Odell shakes his head. "And somehow this qualified?"

"I would consider it a personal tragedy if visitors to our fine town were no longer able to enjoy the world's best french fries." My attempt at wit breaks the tension and he puts an arm around my shoulders.

"Thanks, Mitzy. I guess you can consider it an investment, since you're my best customer."

"Speaking of—" I point to my plate of food. "I better get back to business."

Odell tucks away his emotions and busies himself in the kitchen.

Since Erick and I parted under such intense scrutiny, I didn't really have a chance to ask him how long I should wait. I'm beginning to feel a little uncomfortable, and I'm starting to think that what happened at the station might've been the fever dream of a recently freed hostage.

I take my napkin, wipe my mouth, and I'm just about to bus my own dishes when the front door opens.

At last, one movie trope that doesn't fail is the one when the sparkling sunlight backlights the lead actor and the lead actress turns into a gooey pile of mush on the inside.

I grin stupidly as Erick walks toward me.

He hastily slides into the booth and runs a nervous hand through his hair. This only serves to release a sexy hunk of his blond bangs to hang across one eye and cause my stomach to engage in another round of tingly flip-flops.

"Sorry about that . . . at the station. I—"

"You're sorry?"

For a moment he goes completely still. And then a gorgeous smile spreads across his face like hot syrup on pancakes. "No, I'm not sorry at all."

I grin so hard, I worry the muscles in my cheeks might pop. "That's good to hear."

He licks his lips and tilts his head to the side. "What about you? Are you sorry?"

I'd like to climb up on the table, dance an Irish jig, and scream, "Sorry? Are you kidding me? I've been waiting for this to happen since the day I got to town!" But I've grown up a tiny bit since my arrival in Pin Cherry, and fortunately I choose a more subtle approach. "I'm only sorry it didn't happen sooner."

He blushes adorably and chuckles. "So, I guess the secret's out."

"A secret? In this town? Who do you think you were keeping the secret from?"

He exhales and leans back. "Good point. But it seems like we might've made it official."

My throat goes a little dry and the orphan inside me who's been so careful not to make lasting emotional connections shrinks away in fear.

Even without psychic powers, Erick notices my hesitation. "Am I wrong?" He shrugs. "It's cool if you just want to keep it casual."

Despite his bravado, my extra senses pick up on his true fear of rejection. I take a deep breath and reach my hands across the table to grip his. "Just give my head a little time to catch up with my heart.

I'm not used to letting people in. Not for real, anyway."

The relief that floods through him makes my fingers tingle, and my mood ring flashes me an instant replay of the kiss from the sheriff's station. Boy, I hope that feature is available for later viewing.

Odell slides a steaming plate of meatloaf, mashed potatoes, and gravy in front of Erick, and I pull my hands back to make room. He leans toward Erick and whispers conspiratorially, "You gonna put a restraining order or somethin' on this one?" He jerks his thumb toward me.

I open my mouth to protest, but Erick puts out a hand indicating he'll handle things.

"I don't think a piece of paper signed by a judge is going to do any better job than you and I have. I guess with a woman like her, if you're in for a penny, you're in for a pound."

Odell laughs far too easily, pats Erick on the shoulder, and once again returns to the kitchen shaking his head.

"What's that supposed to mean?"

"It means that you are who you are. An insatiably curious, oddly intelligent, frighteningly accurate, corpse magnet." His laughter fills the diner before he can finish the sentence.

"Rude."

"But true." He picks up a fork and gives me a wink. "Thanks for putting Cleveland and the rest of those SWAT guys in their place. That storage facility is the final piece in the case that's gonna put that gang away for a long, long time."

"Just doin' my CI job, Sheriff."

He chuckles and, by the way his cheeks flush, I'm pretty sure he's remembering more than a business card. "Why don't you fill me in on what happened after they snatched you from Final Destination while I destroy this meatloaf."

I give Erick the same version of the story I gave Deputy Michelson. I add a few additional details about Denny and Breck, since Erick is a friend of Karen's. By the time I finish my tale, he has indeed demolished his meal.

"Seems like you left something out, Moon."

I certainly don't plan on sharing any details of my psychic visions, so I can't imagine what he's talking about. "I don't think so."

"Well then, maybe you can explain why there was a large tan caracal lying on top of my cruiser when I got up this morning."

"Oh, that."

"Yes, that. When I walked into the living room my mother was staring out the front window, mumbling under her breath."

Before you judge a grown man for living with

his mother, I should mention that when Erick got back from Afghanistan he bought his mother a house. She raised him on her own and he wanted to thank her for all the sacrifices she made over the years. Now he does live in that house with her, so technically he lives with his mom. But the fact that he bought her the home and cares for her seems very sweet. I'm sure you'll agree.

"Moon?"

Oops, I slipped away. "She likes cats?" I ask lamely.

He grins. "Anyhow, I walked outside to shoo him off my vehicle and he dropped a rolled-up paper into my hand. Now I'm familiar with all types of secret codes and message transmissions from my time in the Army. I've even heard of carrier pigeons being used to convey information. But I can't say I've ever heard of spy cats."

I chuckle and avoid eye contact.

"When I unrolled the message and discovered it had been written on a page torn from a phonebook with what appeared to be burned matchsticks, it was quite unsettling. Fortunately for you, I had already narrowed down two possible locations for Denny's cabin, and when your note mentioned 'two islands' everything fell into place."

"I wish you could've saved Denny."

"Yeah, he used to be a real good guy. He was

just never the same when he got back. Karen pushed him to get help, but it only caused him to drink more. Sad thing is, I think she would've stuck it out if he hadn't turned on Breck. But every woman has her limits, and that was hers."

"Breck deserves to feel safe."

Erick nods. "It's gonna take some time for him to process all of this."

"For sure." I shake my head and mentally wish them both the best. "Now it's your turn, Sheriff." I wink.

"My turn for what?" He smiles a little too eagerly.

"I don't know what's on your mind, Erick." My attempt at a stern head shake evaporates into a playful wink. "What I meant was that it's your turn to tell me about this 'task force' business."

"Oh, that." He chuckles.

"Yeah. I gotta say I was a little surprised to see the whole train gang in custody."

"Seems like I'll have to award some kind of Honorary Deputy medal to your cat."

My eyes widen and I lean back. "To Pyewacket? For delivering a message?"

"Not exactly. You remember that piece of plastic he swallowed?"

"Yes, of course. I was terrified he wasn't gonna make it."

"Well, I'm glad he did. We could use a guy like him on the force." Erick smiles. "Actually, your dad passed on some information the two of you uncovered during your unauthorized search of the off-limits box cars on the siding."

"We didn't disturb any evidence. And if what you're saying is true, it sounds like we gave you a break in the case."

Erick shakes his head. "Is this how it's always gonna be? Me trying to keep law and order and you trying to squeeze through all the loopholes?" He raises an eyebrow and waits for my reply.

"I hope so."

Erick waves a hand to Odell. "I think we'll take some pie and ice cream if it's not too much trouble."

Odell gives a spatula salute through the orders-up window.

I attempt to return the discussion to my questions. "But seriously, what did Pyewacket and my investigation have to do with anything?"

"We used the tip about the red locks being used to mark the boxcars of the high-ticket items to set up a sting."

Now he has my attention. "A sting? Did you load a bunch of boxcars with empty electronics boxes and then mark them with red locks? Did you place surveillance teams all along the track at two-mile intervals?"

"Nothing that complicated."

I cross my arms. "It wasn't that complicated."

"Since we weren't sure which employee at the depot was leaking information, we made sure your dad had the boxcars loaded and locked as usual. Then, once the train got outside Pin Cherry, it stopped and we replaced all the red locks with yellow. Then we loaded our SWAT team into one of the boxcars and marked it with a red lock." The smug look on Erick's face is far too enticing.

"The ol' Trojan Horse offensive. I love it. Clearly it worked."

"As soon as the train headed up the grade, we heard them clambering along the top of the boxcars. They dropped down and cut the lock. We signaled the conductor to stop the train. As the door rolled open we hurled out several flash grenades and caught most of the crew by surprise. Unfortunately, we took some heavy fire when we approached the two semi trucks waiting on the road below."

I lean forward and suck a worried breath through my teeth.

"A couple guys got winged during the advance and we damaged a 72-inch plasma screen TV that we used as a shield. Thanks to your tip, we had the road blocked in both directions, but an 80,000-pound truck traveling at high speed is pretty likely to make it through any barricade. We were lucky to get everybody in handcuffs before that happened."

"See, I helped."

He slides his hand across the table, grips my fingers, and squeezes. "You could've been killed. No cargo is worth that."

I try and fail to swallow the lump in my throat.

An awkward silence hangs between us. Right on cue, Odell slides our buttery, flaky pin cherry pie with creamy vanilla ice cream onto the table.

We both mutter hasty "thank yous" and dive into our respective desserts to avoid the intense emotions.

"What would you say to a proper date this Saturday?"

The question catches me off guard and I choke on a little bit of my pie as I open my mouth to answer. I grab my napkin and cough into it as the flush of embarrassment swallows me.

Erick smiles. "Feel free to say no, Moon. You don't have to kill yourself to get out of a date." He leans back and crosses his arms in that yummy way that makes his biceps bulge.

I take a long sip of my water and catch my breath. "A date sounds divine." What is it with me and that word? "I'm sure Grams will go nuts picking out an outfit for me." As soon as the words come out of my mouth, I realize my horrible faux pas. My eyes widen and I freeze like a deer in headlights.

A cloud of worry blows across Erick's face. "You mean, she *would* have gone nuts, right?"

I don't dare open my mouth for fear of what might come out, so I simply nod furiously.

He tilts his head and narrows his gaze. "You're a riddle wrapped in an enigma, Moon. But I'll figure out how to unwrap you."

My circuits nearly fry with the imagery that phrase brings to my mind. I take a large scoop of vanilla ice cream and shove it in my mouth, hoping the cool dairy concoction will soothe my fluttering heart.

Erick doesn't seem to hear my racing heart from his side of the table as he devours his pin cherry pie with a smile.

Time for me to take a little advice from *The Gambler* and "know when to walk away." I slip out of the booth, wave to my surrogate-grampa Odell, and give Erick a wink and a finger-gun point.

It's lame, I know, but I'm running on very little sleep, and if I open my mouth I will one hundred percent say something about how I have to get back to the bookshop to update Grams.

Fortunately, he thinks it's one of my adorable quirks and double finger-guns me back as I hurry toward the door.

Grams will be furious that I wasn't wearing heels, but she'll forgive me once I share my swoon-worthy news.

Now all I have to do is figure out a way to keep the sheriff from discovering I see dead people—and stuff.

End of Book 6

But, the mysteries continue...
Curl up with the next book in the Mitzy Moon Mysteries series!

A NOTE FROM TRIXIE

Another case solved! I'll keep writing them if you keep reading . . .

The best part of "living" in Pin Cherry Harbor continues to be feedback from my early readers. Thank you to my alpha readers/cheerleaders Angel and Michael. HUGE thanks to my fantastic beta readers who continue to give me extremely useful and honest feedback: Veronica McIntyre, Renee Arthur, and Nadine Peterse-Vrijhof. And big "small town" hugs to the world's best ARC Team – Trixie's Mystery ARC Detectives!

I can't offer enough praise to my patient and persevering editor Philip Newey! Some authors dread edits, but I always enjoy working with Philip, and I look forward to many more. Any errors are my own.

I would be remiss if I did not mention the influence of my uncle William on my fascination with railroads. Thanks, Uncle.

Now I'm writing book eight in the Mitzy Moon Mysteries series, and I think I may just live in Pin Cherry Harbor forever. Mitzy, Grams, and Pyewacket got into plenty of trouble in book one, *Fries and Alibis*. But I'd have to say that book three, *Wings and Broken Things*, is when most readers say the series becomes unputdownable.

I hope you'll continue to hang out with us.

Trixie Silvertale (April 2020)

SWORDS AND FALLEN LORDS

Mitzy Moon Mysteries 7

A murder in plain sight. A suspect clear as knight. Can this psychic sleuth un-horse the true villain?

Mitzy Moon is no fan of the Renaissance Faire. But her interest is suddenly piqued when a jousting exhibition turns deadly. Following a clue from her magicked mood ring, she's ready to take up the sword and fight for the realm.

Refusing to heed the handsome sheriff's warnings, Mitzy dons a wench's wardrobe and dives into the case. But she'll need the help of her meddling Ghost-ma and spoiled feline to root out the canker. With doxies, scoundrels, and panderers aplenty, it won't be easy to ferret out the truth!

Can Mitzy serve up the knave on a pike, or will she find herself on the wrong end of the lance?

Swords and Fallen Lords is the seventh book in the hilarious paranormal cozy mystery series, Mitzy Moon Mysteries. If you like snarky heroines, supernatural intrigue, and a dash of romance, then you'll love Trixie Silvertale's twisty caper.

Buy *Swords and Fallen Lords* to plunder a whodunit today!

Grab yours here!
readerlinks.com/l/5212001

Scan this QR Code with the camera on your phone. You'll be taken right to the next case!

Once you're in the Club, you'll also be the first to receive updates from Pin Cherry Harbor and access to giveaways, new release announcements, behind-the-scenes secrets, and much more!

Scan this QR Code with the camera on your phone. You'll be taken right to the page to join the Club!

THANK YOU!

Trying out a new book is always a risk and I'm thankful that you rolled the dice with Mitzy Moon. If you loved the book, the sweetest thing you can do (*even sweeter than pin cherry pie à la mode*) is to leave a review so that other readers will take a chance on Mitzy and the gang.

Don't feel you have to write a book report. A brief comment like, "Can't wait to read the next book in this series!" will help potential readers make their choice.

Leave a quick review HERE
https://readerlinks.com/l/1033892

Thank you kindly, and I'll see you in Pin Cherry Harbor!

Mitzy Moon Mysteries

Paranormal Cozy Mysteries

Fries and Alibis

Tattoos and Clues

Wings and Broken Things

Sparks and Landmarks

Charms and Firearms

Bars and Boxcars

Swords and Fallen Lords

Wakes and High Stakes

Tracks and Flashbacks

Lies and Pumpkin Pies

Hopes and Slippery Slopes

Hearts and Dark Arts

Dames and Deadly Games

Castaways and Longer Days

Schemes and Bad Dreams

Carols and Yule Perils

Dangers and Empty Mangers

Heists and Poltergeists

Blades and Bridesmaids

Scones and Tombstones

Vandals and Yule Scandals

Harper and Moon Investigations
Paranormal Cozy Mysteries

Ropes and Last Hopes

Bells and Bombshells

Rodeo Clowns and Shakedowns

Stiffs and Petroglyphs

Fatal Wines and Valentines

April Curses and May Hearses

Wheels and Dirty Deals

Scripts and Empty Crypts

Christmas Catastrophe Mysteries
Culinary Cozy Mysteries

Peppermint Cookie Murder

Apple Dumpling Murder

Linzer Cookie Murder

Chocolate Crinkle Cookie Murder

...more to come!

MAGICAL RENAISSANCE FAIRE MYSTERIES

Explore the world of Coriander the Conjurer. A fortune-telling fairy with a heart of gold!

 Book 1:

All Swell That Ends Spell – A dubious festival. A fatal swim. Can this fortune-telling fairy herald the true killer?

 Book 2:

Fairy Wives of Windsor – A jolly Faire. A shocking murder. Can this furtive fairy outsmart the killer?

 Book 3:

Double Double Royal Trouble – When a treat-peddling witch is found dead, will this cursed faire crumble?

Join Sydney Coleman and her unruly ghosts, as they solve mysteries in a truly haunted mansion!

Book 1: ***Moonlight and Mischief*** – She's desperate for a fresh start, but is a mansion on sale too good to be true?

Book 2: ***Moonlight and Magic*** – A haunted Halloween tour seem like the perfect plan, until there's murder…

Book 3: ***Moonlight and Mayhem*** – An unwelcome visitor. A surprising past. Will her fire sale end in smoke?

ABOUT THE AUTHOR

USA TODAY Bestselling author Trixie Silvertale grew up reading an endless supply of Lilian Jackson Braun, Hardy Boys, and Nancy Drew novels. She loves the amateur sleuths in cozy mysteries and obsesses about all things paranormal. Those two passions unite in all her cozy mysteries, and she's thrilled to write them and share them with you.

When she's not consumed by writing, she bakes to fuel her creative engine and pulls weeds in her herb garden to clear her head (*and sometimes she pulls out her hair, but mostly weeds*).

Greetings are welcome:
trixie@trixiesilvertale.com

f facebook.com/TrixieSilvertale
instagram.com/trixiesilvertale
BB bookbub.com/authors/trixie-silvertale

www.ingramcontent.com/pod-product-compliance
Lightning Source LLC
Chambersburg PA
CBHW022000170626
46808CB00001B/230